Hide and Seek

H. L. Wegley

HIDE AND SEEK

Contact Information: titleadmin@pelicanbookgroup.com

Cover Art by Nicola Martinez

Harbourlight Books, a division of Pelican Ventures, LLC
www.pelicanbookgroup.com PO Box 1738 *Aztec, NM * 87410

Harbourlight Books sail and mast logo is a trademark of Pelican Ventures, LLC

Publishing History
First Harbourlight Edition, 2013
Print Edition ISBN 978-1-61116-203-5
Electronic Edition ISBN 978-1-61116-202-8
Published in the United States of America

Dedication

This book is dedicated to my wife, Babe, who was the inspiration for the character and personality of Jennifer.

How does a story residing in the heart and mind of a writer become a published book? With the help of a lot of talented people. I want to thank those talented people who helped me.

First, I thank my wife, Babe, who patiently suffered through countless versions of the novel while serving as my main sounding board. Thanks also to my test readers, Duke Gibson, Dallas Mickey, Jill and Brett Lloyd, who endured the pain of reading an unpolished draft of my very first novel.

Thanks, Brett, for also serving as my technical advisor for law-enforcement issues, weapons and explosives.

A special thanks to the talented David Boyett for his voice-over in the book trailer.

Many thanks to the Pelican Book Group team, especially to my editor, Jamie West, and Editor-in-Chief, Nicola Martinez, who designed the book cover.

A very special thank you to the critique group at American Christian Fiction Writers who critiqued the manuscript and unselfishly shared their knowledge.

Finally, thanks to our Lord, Who revealed Himself to us in stories, and Who gives us the privilege of revealing Him to others in our stories.

1

6:00 a.m. Saturday, March 18

Never practice unwise behavior.

Lee Brandt made that vow as a teenager the same year he swore off dating. Now, here he was thirteen years later parked on a secluded road with a member of the opposite sex.

I really hate irony.

He glanced at the woman sitting in the driver's seat. Jennifer Akihara was the most beautiful woman he'd ever met. She was also the most intelligent. Most guys would die to be sitting here on this Western-Washington mountain road with Jennifer. When he glanced into the passenger-side mirror, it appeared likely that he would.

A vehicle slowed on the highway, and a blast of air left his lungs.

Jennifer's gaze froze on the rearview mirror and she gasped.

Those lights had pursued them most of the night.

The vehicle turned towards them.

That sent his heart racing.

In an instant, their dead-end hideout turned into a trap.

Jennifer cut the engine and Lee took her hand. Despite the rising panic, awareness of their first touch etched an indelible mark in his memory. The early light of dawn revealed her wide-eyed fear mingled with something he couldn't interpret.

He refocused on her face. He had put her in danger, so he had to keep her alive, whatever it took.

He tugged on her hand. "Slide out on my side, Jenn. Don't leave any obvious footprints. If they think we ran up the road, it'll buy us a few minutes. We're going up the mountain, instead."

Lee released her hand and leaned out the open door. By standing on the door frame, he could peer over a small rise all the way to the highway. Towering above the car, he monitored the progress of the approaching vehicle, still nearly a mile away.

"Wait 'til I'm over the console." Jennifer slid to her right. "I'm over it."

"OK, let's go."

They leaped from the bullet-riddled sedan onto the grass beside the road and ran towards the steep mountain slope. In less than three minutes, the gunmen would reach her car. In another minute, the goons would probably find their trail. Then the race up the mountain would begin.

Lee needed every second of that time to build a buffer that would keep them out of sight and out of gunshot range.

To get his bearings, he glanced towards the southeast shoulder of the large limestone spire perched on the mountaintop. A hidden cave he found there as a kid—one of many caves—would become their hiding place.

Or our tomb.

If it became a tomb, all knowledge of the threat they had uncovered last night would be entombed with them. That was the intent of the terrorists, drug-cartel members—whoever the gunmen chasing them actually were.

Jennifer, the graduate student Dr. Martin sent to help Lee investigate the computer security breach, was incredible. She was long on brains and beauty. Slender and small, she appeared a little short on what they needed now, brawn. Should he treat her like a little sister, or like—as much as he wanted to, he didn't have time to think about that now.

He offered his hand to her.

She took it without hesitation.

He pulled her through the roadside bushes, avoiding the thorny berry vines now visible in the dawn.

"Be careful, Lee," Jennifer spoke softly, slightly breathless, as they ran hand-in-hand towards the mountain. "Yanking me off my feet will only slow us down."

"Sorry." He'd lost his focus. He adjusted his stride to match Jennifer's. "Tell me if I'm going too fast. But run hard. We've got to get to the trees."

He dismissed the fear in her eyes. After her gutsy night driving, he knew she was game. She could perform under pressure.

Dr. Martin said she had an Einstein-level IQ. Lee guessed with people like Jennifer self-reliance died hard. Was God-reliance ever born?

They broke through the last of the brush near the base of the mountain and entered the forest. Towering Douglas firs dominated all other vegetation, the trunks providing their only protection. They needed to keep a lot of tree trunks between them and the goons, at least three or four hundred yards. If even one green laser beam reached them…

He shoved the thought from his mind and tried to focus on something positive. But a horrifying video intruded, playing repeatedly. Green beams of light danced all over Jennifer's body.

"No!" he protested.

"What is it?" she huffed.

"Nothing. It's OK." He squeezed her hand. "Just keep running. Don't hold back. When you're tired, I'll help."

"I'm already tired. They chased us all night."

"It will get harder before it gets easier. Don't give up. I know we can make it."

She didn't reply.

That was lame. He'd meant to encourage her.

As the sun topped the Cascades to the east, car doors slammed in rapid succession in the small valley below. He pulled her to a stop.

"How many doors did you hear?"

"Not sure…three, I think." She squeezed the words between heavy breaths.

"Three of them," he concluded, hoping he wouldn't have to make a life-or-death decision based on his unverified assumption.

They broke into a run, but Jennifer struggled to maintain the pace.

Lee glanced back periodically to monitor her ebbing strength.

Over the last several yards, the slope steepened and Jennifer slowed from a jog to a walk.

He needed to start helping her.

"Wait a second, Jenn." He pulled her to a stop again and craned his neck to look up through the trees. They hid the limestone spire. Maybe the trees would also hide them. Maybe Jennifer could make it farther before he had to pull her weight. Maybe they would make it safely — *too many maybes.*

He gave her as much rest as he dared, and then tugged on her hand. "Come on. We need to get to the first rock outcropping."

They jogged up the mountainside, but Jennifer struggled on the steep slope.

He wasn't doing much better. When he tried to speak, his sentences came in staccato bursts of words, chopped apart by gasps. "Jenn, give me...your left...hand." He reached back with his right and they locked hands around the wrists. "Hold on tight...stay on...your feet."

"I'll try. But one of us...must contact the FBI...I'm slowing you down so—"

"Don't even think that...I'll help you...we'll make it." He began pulling more of her weight.

Jennifer stumbled behind him. "Are you sure this is the best—"

"There are caves up there...I played here as a kid...we can hide...they won't find us...I'll keep you safe." He said the words, but did he still believe them? He glanced at the steep slope. They had about three-eighths of a mile to go. Nearly a thousand feet in elevation to climb.

They needed to run. Even rested he wasn't in that kind of shape. He hadn't a clue if Jennifer ever had been. Adrenaline sometimes accomplished amazing things, but with their lives on the line they could use some help from another source, a source Jennifer said she doubted. Her agnosticism was another reason he needed to keep her safe.

They hit the breakpoint where the slope steepened to a few degrees shy of a cliff.

In thirty seconds, the slope claimed his legs. In another ten seconds, it took everything else. He tried praying again, but chase scenes and bullets from the previous evening disrupted his thoughts, becoming reruns of the horror movie they were cast in a few hours earlier. The reruns ended with the green lights dancing on Jennifer's body.

To force the images from his mind, he focused on Jennifer.

If the gunmen gained on them, fear might paralyze her as much as exhaustion.

He needed to keep her calm and confident.

Like me.

"Yeah, right," he mumbled to himself between breaths that grew more labored, raspy, and inadequate by the second.

Below them, cracking brush told him the gunmen had reached the base of the mountain.

They had at least a three-hundred-yard lead.

Not four hundred, but it would have to do.

A jerk on his arm nearly pulled him off his feet. He looked back.

Jennifer had stopped.

He pulled on her arm to continue their climb.

She leaned forward, trying to step ahead, but her legs didn't move.

He stopped pulling. If she fell and twisted an ankle—*I can't let that happen or we're dead.* He stepped close and gripped her upper arm with both hands to support more of her weight. "Jenn...if you...want to live...keep going."

Jennifer moved sporadically and stopped responding.

He wasn't doing much better. His lungs burned, as

his oxygen debt threatened to bankrupt him. This wasn't working. Would he have to carry her?

He needed to concentrate, but his mind went fuzzy. He stumbled to his right, pulling Jennifer with him.

They stood at the edge of a gap in the trees. When he looked down the narrow clearing, he became vaguely aware of the extent of the gap. Far below, he detected movement.

The belching of automatic weapons startled him. Just below them, flying dirt exploded into the air. It created two parallel lines running up the hill, converging on Jennifer.

Two green spots of light moved onto her body.

No!

He yanked her to the left.

She cried out.

They fell in a tangle of arms and legs and rolled into the cover of fir trees.

The lines of death continued up the hillside for a few yards. Then the shooting stopped.

Jennifer lay still beside him, eyes closed. But she was breathing.

He clenched his jaw and looked at her legs. He expected to see blood-soaked jeans, or worse. No blood. He thanked God.

With the force of a sledge hammer, the thought of what had nearly happened drove a spike deep into the pit of his stomach. He pulled Jennifer's body close and held her, as if somehow that would protect her. The shots had missed them, but if he'd remained vigilant, there would have been no shots. "I'm so sorry, Jenn...my fault...won't happen again."

Jennifer replied only with deep, gasping breaths.

As he held her, conflicting emotions mushroomed out of control, hatred for those who'd nearly killed her, and something else—something entirely different.

Please help me keep her safe.

Would she still trust him enough to follow his lead? He held her tightly, trying to protect her body with his for...he didn't know how long. Regardless, it was longer than they could afford.

Her brown, almond-shaped eyes opened, and Lee peered into them, trying to read anything they revealed. He saw fatigue and something else. Was it trust? He couldn't read her well. She seemed to mask things.

"Is your arm OK?" He had jerked so hard he wondered if he'd dislocated her shoulder.

"I'll...survive," she whispered through a deep breath.

"We both will." His voice didn't sound convincing.

She leaned to one side, supporting herself with the shoulder in question.

He pulled her gently to her feet and drew her farther back into the cover of the trees. "If you see me start to do something stupid again, Jenn...just tell me."

She didn't reply.

He took her hand and tried pulling her up the hill.

She didn't respond. Her head sagged forward. Her shoulders drooped. One of her knees buckled, and she almost fell.

Please, not now. It's not that much farther.

"Hang in there, we're almost there." He changed direction, traveling parallel to the slope. Immediately strength returned to the muscles in his legs. Maybe this respite meant they could catch their breaths before resuming the climb.

His maneuver also disguised his intended destination, the concealed cave. If they reached the spire and slipped into the cave before their pursuers arrived, the gunmen could never find them. If...

After they moved steadily along the contours of the slope for nearly two hundred yards, Jennifer spoke for the first time in several minutes. "I'm OK now. Let's go, Lee."

He tried to give her an encouraging smile. "It's not far now. One more burst of speed and those thugs are toast."

"Me too...of a heart attack," she panted. A faint smile appeared on her lips. Jennifer would never voluntarily give up. "But, Lee...you'd better be right about...where we're going... or I'll kill you."

He squeezed her hand. "If I'm wrong...you won't have to."

That was brilliant, Lee. You idiot!

He led Jennifer parallel to the slope for several minutes.

Her drooping posture soon disappeared. She quickened her pace and moved to his side, putting her hand on his shoulder. "Lee, I really am OK, now."

Stopping for a moment, he glanced through the trees. He could see rocks. Lowering his gaze, he looked into her eyes.

The vibrant, intelligent Jennifer was back. She really was OK.

Full of life again, her gaze drove away the despair threatening to drown him. Hope flowed in, replacing it.

"Then it's time to move up to the limestone formation."

They reached the first limestone outcropping, a hundred yards below the tall spire.

If we're going to lose these guys, this is where it starts.

"We'll be on rocks most of the time, now," he whispered. "There's a lot of moss on them. Don't kick any of it loose. Don't kick any rocks loose, either. They create noisy little avalanches. Avoid patches of bare dirt."

"I get the point, Lee. Make it hard for them to track us."

"Yeah. And we'll change direction a few times to disguise where we're headed. Ready?"

"So, we'll be going more slowly, now?"

"Definitely. We used our brawn to get here."

"What brawn?"

"How much do you think?"

"All of it." She rolled her eyes.

He grinned. "You got that right. But it was enough."

She sent him a warm smile.

He resisted the strong urge to hold her and reassure her. Instead, he turned to look at the spire. "OK. If the brawn's all gone, it's time to use our brains to shake these guys for good."

"Let's use yours. Mine's too tired right now." She smiled again, and trust filled her eyes.

It placed a heavy burden on him, but it also made his spirit soar. Completing the climb bought them precious time. His tension level ratcheted down several notches as their high-stakes game morphed from run-for-your-life to hide-and-seek. All kids knew when they hid they needed to make sure the person counting to one hundred wasn't peeking.

Crashing noises and the clatter of rolling rocks

erupted below.

From down there the goons couldn't possibly peek.

Jennifer grabbed his hand, squeezing tightly. "That sounds close. Are we still OK? They aren't—"

"We're doing fine," he whispered. "They're not tracking us very well. In fact, it sounds like they're moving away from us, to our right."

Soon it would become much harder to see any tracks. Eventually their trail would disappear.

They would hide, and the goons would seek in vain.

At least that's what he planned.

Lee hadn't planned the events of the previous twenty-four hours. Accidentally wandering onto the turf of terrorists, evil could envelop one before one was even aware of its presence.

Though it seemed like everything happened in the last day, in reality, the roots of this deadly drama went back more than four months. From the roots, a story grew. It was a story he would never forget. But he had two questions.

How long would the story last?

And how would it end?

2

November 15, four months earlier

"It's insane!"

Lee pounded the desk with his fist, knocking his outstanding-performance award to the floor. When he swiveled his chair to pick it up, his gaze caught the brass nameplate on his cubicle wall, Lee Brandt, DEDS System Architect.

It sounded impressive. He thought so, too, until his boss at National Aerospace, Barry Lafferty, had made the announcement a few minutes ago. The Digital Engineering Data System, DEDS, was about to become the Digital Engineering Data outsourced System.

As Lee grabbed his award, Dave Rothermel, a fellow worker on the DEDS project, stepped into his cubicle. "Did I just hear the word, insane?"

Lee studied him.

Dave's pursed lips replaced his usual smile.

"Yes, it's insane." He used what he intended to make the catchphrase of his evangelistic campaign to save the soul of the project.

"If it's any consolation, I agree with you, Lee. That's partly why I intend to move on."

Of course, Dave would bail. Like all hard-core programmers, Dave's work philosophy was simple, write code, or shrivel up and die. Writing specifications and doing acceptance testing—that was not Dave.

It wasn't Lee, either.

"Other than being insane, what's your take on the outsourcing of our system, and what do you intend to do?"

"For now, I'm going to stay and try to prevent the management of National Aerospace from selling national security down the drain."

Dave frowned. "Isn't that a bit melodramatic? I'm leaving because I want to write code, not functional specifications. Why all the gloom and doom about national security?"

"We have everything from publicly available data, to proprietary data, and even classified data. Of course, we maintain separate commercial and military environments for the system, but we can't give Bangalore Business Technologies access to all that data."

"No, we can't. But we'll define all of it for them in the functional specs."

"My point is…that's not enough." Lee's voice sounded harsh, even to himself. "You can't develop a working system—one that is so data-driven—from only a specification. To test their code, the BBT developers will need the actual data—all the data anomalies for all categories: National Aerospace proprietary, NOFORN, ITAR, and some of the classified data."

Dave shook his head. "We won't put that data in the development and test environment. We might dummy it up, but we'll never give them the real stuff."

Lee clenched his teeth. "Not until all heck breaks loose, like it's sure to do when the new DEDS fails acceptance testing. Do you know where the system is going to break, Dave?"

"Probably while trying to process some of our weird proprietary data on the commercial side, or the classified-data anomalies when we host the system on the defense side of the house in their environment."

"You got that right." Lee shook his head and stared at the floor. "When the pressure is on to fix the problems"—he looked up into Dave's face—"what do you think will happen?"

"What else, the CEO will get involved—you know...to rescue the contract—the insane contract that was his idea, as was his misguided outsourcing initiative."

Lee stood. "And that's when security will take a backseat to expediency." Lee stepped towards Dave, and his voice increased in volume to somewhere between forte and fortissimo. "There will be security breaches...mark my words!"

Dave stepped back. "Lee, I know you're frustrated. But you need to be careful, or you could lose your job." He paused. "But you're right about security. Two of our competitors were hit with fines and penalties last year for security infringements on outsourced systems, ones that went to offshore firms."

"See what I mean." Lee's voice dropped a few decibels. "It's insane."

****

Lee started preaching the gospel of insanity to anyone who would listen. A few days later, when he verbalized his catchphrase to a reporter in the parking lot, it appeared on the front page of the area's biggest newspaper.

Barry stormed into Lee's cubicle and threatened to remove "System Architect" from his nameplate.

After Barry left his cubicle, Dave stepped in. "Don't forget what I said. You could actually lose your job. Barry's the kind of guy who would fire his best friend if he thought it would get him to the next rung on the corporate ladder. But...I found a job."

Lee sighed. "Don't mind me. It's been a bad morning. But about the job—that's great. Where will you be working?"

"Over at plant three...with the Laser Technology Team. Are you still planning to stay on the project?"

"I think so, at least for now. I'll stay, write specifications, and watch the BBT contractors like a hawk."

Dave extended his hand to Lee. "Well, goodbye."

Lee shook it. "You'll do well over there. Write some code for me."

3

March 17

Lee sat at his desk drumming his fingers and shaking his head. When the work started last November, he'd predicted security breaches. Did he really want security to be compromised just so he could say, 'I told you so?' He would plead the fifth to that question.

Barry's head appeared over the cubicle partition. "Lee, the contractors don't understand this spec. You need to make it a little more...user friendly. I've got to run. Have a meeting in a few minutes."

Barry dropped some stapled papers onto Lee's desk and disappeared.

Lee picked up the functional specification and began to read. He was soon deep into the process of revising the spec to reflect the underlying system requirements while using a restricted subset of the English language for the contractors' benefit.

This is insane. I'm a computer scientist, not a linguist.

Lee's phone rang, shattering his already impaired concentration. "Hello, Lee Brandt here."

"Lee, this is Joe at Computing Security. I need you to come to my office as soon as possible. Barry's here, too. We have a problem."

"I'm on my way over."

If Joe was concerned, there must be bad news for

somebody. He closed the session on his server, locked his desktop, and walked downstairs to Joe's office. The door was open, so he stepped in.

"Before you say I told you so, just listen to Joe for a minute. OK?" Barry said, his expression grim.

"Yeah, sure." Lee's conscience winced at the tone of his voice. He knew he should treat Barry with more respect, even if his boss didn't always deserve it. "So what's the problem?"

Joe motioned for Lee to sit down. "This is the scenario we're dealing with. We believe one of our foreign contractors got into some data they shouldn't have been able to see. At this point, we're not sure whose fault it is—"

"I told you—"

"I know very well what you told me." Joe's voice grew loud, out of character for him.

"It's insane—pure insanity."

Barry glared at him. "That's enough, Lee. Will you please shut up, and listen to Joe?"

Though he'd lost his composure, Lee knew when to back off. He folded his hands on the table and waited to hear the bad news.

Joe let out a long sigh. "One of your co-workers, Ron Hemsworth, left his cell at work. When he came in late last evening, he walked by the B-size printer and saw a restricted drawing in the output bin, the printer that the contractors use in development.

"We think there may have been a paper jam and when someone cleared it, the drawing printed a second time—that print server's a bit flaky. When Hemsworth—"

"Leaving a print behind—that sounds pretty sloppy if someone here is actually involved in industrial espionage or ripping off restricted data. Whoever it was could have checked the print queue to make sure they left nothing behind, and then we would have never known about the breach." Lee began running other scenarios through his mind.

Joe continued. "As I was saying, Hemsworth found an ITAR-restricted drawing in the output bin of that printer, military-related data we have to protect from access by all foreign nationals. Before you say anything, I know that particular drawing should not have been in the insecure development environment, and I was assured there would be no ITAR data in development. It was a stipulation of the contract with BBT. But that's a separate issue which I'm currently working on."

Joe paused and met Lee's gaze. "What Barry and I need to know is if any other unauthorized data have been accessed, ITAR or, heaven forbid, classified data. Lee, we need you to find out who accessed what on the development system between February 21 and March 15. Now…how long is it going to take you to do that?"

On the surface this seemed the fulfillment of Lee's data-breach prophecy. Or were they being snookered? He would reserve judgment until he analyzed the logs. "I can have the initial analysis to you by tomorrow evening. But have you considered there may be a lot more to this than just one of our Indian contractors looking at one ITAR drawing?"

"We'd rather not think about that eventuality." Joe paused. "Yes, we've considered it. We'll cross that bridge if, and when, we come to it."

"Lee, I don't want to hear any more disrespectful talk about the contractors. Understood?" Barry spoke, his expression grim.

"Yes, I understand." Lee knew there were some very talented people among the contractors, but he couldn't help resenting their presence. They were doing work that was rightfully his. Perhaps they were taking things not rightfully theirs in the process.

"Now, do you have everything you need to do this analysis? Equipment, people, and—"

"I have all the resources I need." Lee cut in. "I have my own server and my repository of reusable scripts, so I'll get started now. If I need any help, you'll be the first to know." Lee's conscience prodded him sharply upon uttering his last statement. He would go to nearly anyone for help before he would turn to Barry.

He stood, hoping that would end the meeting. He wanted to get started. If he could just come up with some hard facts that said, "I told you so," that might provide some job satisfaction.

"Then why don't we plan on meeting in my office again on Monday morning at 9:00 a.m.?" Joe stood up. "You'll have the entire weekend if you need it."

Just take my entire weekend and then pretend you've done me a favor.

"How nice of you, Joe. I'll see you guys Monday morning." He felt another twinge of conscience. As a Christian, he must show respect for the positions of authority Joe and Barry held. It was a fine line, a line Lee sometimes wobbled off like a drunk taking a sobriety test.

Walking back from the meeting, Lee wondered if he should start looking for a job in meteorology. He held a BS in meteorology and worked as a weather officer in the Air Force. Two of his friends, Dale and Jerry, were wooing him to join their start-up weather-consulting firm, but they…

He needed to quit daydreaming and get focused on the task at hand.

He had built a research-oriented, logging system and used it to archive detailed, system-usage records. Since he ran the same data-logging software in the development environment, he would use the data collected there to finger the rat who'd accessed unauthorized data through a hole probably created when populating the development environment with test data. It was a rat hole the CEO and his henchmen made possible by outsourcing a critical system. It was a rat hole that should never…

He needed to stop his internal ranting. He needed to do a lot of things. Leaving this project was probably one of them.

Back at his desk, Lee unlocked his desktop, opened a session on his server, along with his favorite programmer's editor. In the editor, he began cobbling together a script he named Ratfinger.

Don't worry, little guy. I'll make sure you know how to finger a rat.

Two hours later, Lee closed the editor, saving the program in the process. After a short, successful test run, he was satisfied with his work. At the command-line prompt, he told Ratfinger to go fulfill its destiny.

Lee glanced at the clock. 5:15 p.m. Knowing the script might run for a couple of hours, he reviewed everything he knew about the twelve contractors from BBT. He wasn't in management, so he couldn't peruse BBT's Human Resources records. Résumés and chat time with the contractors were his only resources.

All twelve were most recently from Bangalore. He knew that four were Muslim and eight were Hindu. He had talked a little religion with them.

All twelve had several years experience in information technology and at least a BS in Computer Science. There was nothing in those facts that pointed towards anyone committing espionage. For now, that job would remain delegated to Ratfinger.

As his script sorted through gigabytes of data, Lee sorted out the sources of discontent with his current job. The events of the last several months caused him to regret jumping ship from his career as a meteorologist to pursue mainstream computer-science work.

Forecasting power for an array of wind turbines or issuing warnings for a blizzard in North Dakota seemed more rewarding to him than writing systems code for a Fortune 500 aerospace company under their continually severe time and funding constraints.

The atmosphere could be a fickle and unfaithful paramour, often turning against a forecaster when they least expected it. But taming commercial systems development was worse than any words Lee voluntarily allowed into his vocabulary.

Much sooner than he expected, a window popped up on his monitor, interrupting his musings. The script had finished. Simultaneously, the big laser printer in the corner started spitting out paper. He walked towards the printer, praying it would prove to be a rat trap.

The report he pulled from the printer was a bit crude, but it contained all the required information. Since he was the only one who would have to read it, it would suffice. The million-dollar question. Did Ratfinger live up to its name?

Lee spread the printed report across his desk,

lining up the data columns on each adjacent page. He started scanning down the column for ITAR-restricted drawings, one category of military information not authorized for disclosure to foreigners. Four drawings were accessed, all by contract employee number five.

So there is some dirty work going on. I'd bet money all of it was done by one person.

The classified-data category was next. There should have been no classified data on the insecure development system, but he couldn't make that assumption. Consequently, he'd programmed the script to verify the security category by performing a cross-check, using another company database. With that check, the program would never cry wolf. Mindful of Ratfinger's veracity, he ran his finger down the classified-data column. His finger stopped near the bottom. Someone accessed one classified drawing. Once again, it was contractor number five, Ramesh Nath. He'd found his rat.

Lee quickly logged in to his database manager's account and put a Band-Aid on the problem. He removed all access to the classified drawing.

How classified data ended up in the development environment was another question for another time. Joe only asked Lee to determine who'd accessed what. But Joe hadn't explicitly forbidden him from delving further. He wanted the goods on this person.

Should I probe deeper?

Stupid question.

If things went awry, he might have to beg for forgiveness later, but right now, he wanted to contact Ram without disclosing what he knew and to see how Ram reacted to a few pointed questions sprinkled randomly throughout their conversation.

The contact list for project employees was posted on the DEDS project website. But when he checked there, Lee found Ram wasn't listed. Since it was after hours, he looked up the home phone for the Indian contractor's program manager and keyed the number into his personal cell phone.

"Hi, Ash, this is Lee Brandt. Sorry to bother you after work hours, but do you have the phone number for Ram? It's not on the project website."

"I took it off because Ramesh flew back to Bangalore two days ago. We do not expect him to return to the project."

Lee put his index finger on his desk calendar. "So he left on the fifteenth?"

Got out of Dodge the day after the classified drawing was accessed.

"That's right. Do you want me to call my supervisor and put you in touch with him?"

He shook his head. "No, no, that's OK. You don't need to call anyone else."

"I hope that his departure causes no problems."

"No, no problems. Thanks."

It did cause one problem. The rat ran before he could finger him.

Certainly there was more to this incident than simply an unauthorized person accessing a classified drawing. Ram viewed and printed a classified, radar-antenna-assembly installation drawing for a National Aerospace bomber, making him appear guilty of espionage. And then Ram left for home.

Once there, he would likely never be found, or prosecuted. Ram's profit from selling the classified document couldn't be much. The drawing was classified, but it revealed no big secrets. However, because of Ram's crime, BBT could lose their multi-million dollar contract with National Aerospace. It was a huge risk for so little gain.

The whole breach scenario was illogical, or stupid, unless Ram was an agent for someone other than his employer. If so, he had a more sinister motive than small-time espionage.

Lee glanced at the clock. It was nearly 6 p.m. and he was alone in the lab. He grabbed his flash drive with all his portable freeware tools on it and walked across the room to Ram's National-Aerospace-issued laptop, still docked on Ram's desk. He logged in as administrator. With great expectations, he inserted his flash drive.

National Aerospace computer policies prohibited installation of unauthorized software on company computers. Running portable versions of unauthorized programs from a flash drive obeyed the letter of the law, but certainly not the spirit. But solving the mystery was important to National Aerospace, and possibly, to national security.

His portable applications manager popped open on the screen, and from it, Lee opened a program enabling him to trace network communications. But in the tray he saw the VPN client's icon appear. Employees used this client to login to National Aerospace's virtual private network when they worked off-site. But evidently logging on to the laptop had started the VPN client.

Strange. That wasn't how National Aerospace's VPN client was configured to work. The employee had to initiate it explicitly and use a special key to gain access.

Ram, because he was a foreign national, was not

given an account to use the VPN client. While Ram's behavior was a little bit fishy, his computer's behavior appeared malevolent.

Had Ram hacked the VPN client? If so, what "enhancements" had he added? Who was the VPN client actually communicating with? And what was it transmitting?

Lee looked at the ports in use. On several pairs of ports, the laptop was communicating with some machine outside the company—ports that shouldn't be used for these purposes. This wasn't standard company software. Furthermore, two of the remote-host IP addresses—located in Texas and Colorado—were in states where National Aerospace had no employees.

Ram, what are you up to?

Convinced some sort of malware was loaded onto the laptop, Lee ran a full-system virus scan. While the scan iterated through the files on the laptop, he rummaged through the system files looking for malware, but saw nothing out of the ordinary. When the virus scan came back clean, he had exhausted his analytical resources.

He was going to need some help.

He decided to call his old friend and mentor, Dr. Howard Martin, at the university. Howie worked well into the evening when doing research. He taught computer security courses and did a lot of contract research, most recently for the FBI, DHS, and NSA— the kind of folks Lee could use right now. He pressed Howie's entry on his cell-phone.

"Hello, this is Dr. Martin."

"Howie, this is Lee Brandt. I've got a computer-security issue over here. The problem is with a contractor's company-issued laptop."

"Is the contractor there with you?"

"No. He left the country a short time ago—in a big hurry. It's all very suspicious."

"So you need someone to help you check out his machine?"

"Yes. I need to locate a well-hidden Trojan virus that's communicating through our firewalls, and I need to know who's on the other end. And, Howie, I need the help tonight."

"Can you come over to my office at the university?"

"Sure, I can be there in fifteen minutes."

"Good. I'll have someone who can help you."

"Thanks. See you in a few minutes."

Why did Howie want him to come to the U? Sometimes the man had undisclosed motives which didn't become apparent until later. Lee needed a break, so he was glad to accommodate his professor.

Lee walked to the parking lot and hopped into his blue, '65 Mustang convertible, his baby. When the 289, with its racing cam, began its sweet, syncopated rumble, a grin spread across his face. He slipped the performance automatic transmission into gear and headed north towards the University District and hopefully towards Howie's cyber-sleuth.

4

Jennifer Akihara stood in front of the corkboard mounted on the computer lab wall, poring over the large drawing pinned there. She'd drawn it to depict her highly abstracted, comprehensive view of Internet topology. Annotated with numerous mathematical expressions, the drawing looked like an incomprehensible hodgepodge to most people, but this tool enabled her to visualize new heuristics—complex rules of thumb applicable to certain classes of intractable problems. Using some of these heuristics, she had devised algorithms that isolated patterns of Internet communication. These algorithms could be tuned to recognize networks of terrorists, criminals, and other groups of interest to law enforcement, the military, and the intelligence community.

That's why she received the job offer she held in her hand, the one from NSA, the latest of a seemingly endless stream of job offers from potential employers she'd been receiving since she was in high school.

This hadn't been a particularly productive day, and Jennifer's mind craved action, rather than the application of theory. She turned around when the lab door clicked open.

Howie gave her a goofy smile.

She recognized the look. He had something up his sleeve.

But Howie's smile also reminded her of all he had

done for her during her master's program. The pain of her memories didn't come as often now, but she wouldn't have made it through the past two years after her father's death without Howie subbing as her father. She owed him a great debt of gratitude for all he he'd done for her while she grieved.

"I just found out there's someone who desperately needs your help. Right now, if you have the time."

"Who, Howie?"

"National Aerospace. There was an apparent security breach involving a foreign contractor and his company-issued laptop."

"I thought you said someone...you know...a person, needed my help." Jennifer mulled it over. National Aerospace was a government contractor. This could turn out to be something serious. "Can you tell me a little more about it?"

"A laptop is communicating out through the National Aerospace firewall and they suspect there's some malevolent software on it. But we'll know more soon. Lee Brandt, one of my former students, will be here shortly to brief us."

"I'll help if I can. We certainly don't want National Aerospace falling victim to hackers."

"Good. Thanks. Lee is a good guy and you're the best person to help him with..." Howie's words continued as the door closed behind him, but the hum of air conditioning and computing equipment drowned them.

Howie knew about her trouble with obsessive men. He knew why she preferred to hide among the computer nerds and geeks. They respected her for her skills, not for how good they thought she looked.

Lee is a good guy?

Was Howie trying to set up his "adopted" daughter with a suitable young man?

Hopefully not. She wasn't ready for that. Merely associating with one had lead to danger. That's why she kept the Smith & Wesson .38 Special in her purse.

That was also why she became an expert marksman...with one notch already on her gun.

****

When Lee walked into Howie's office, he stifled a laugh at the incongruity between the clean, dust-free office, with every book on the shelves in its place, while two dozen foot-high stacks of journals, articles, and research notes lay distributed irregularly across the floor. But that was Howie. A study in paradoxes. He was a brilliant computer scientist, yet he tried to play the father role for every grad student in his charge.

"Grab a chair, Lee. We have the best person in America to help you with your...uh...problem. Absolutely brilliant." Howie's eyes lit like neon lights.

"Great. Is it anyone I know?"

"No, Lee, I don't think you know her."

Her?

Lee's defenses leapt to high alert—DEFCON 2. He was primed and ready to go to war. The last time he worked with a younger female student she was more interested in a romantic relationship than accomplishing the goals of the team-based master's project. He'd barely managed a satisfactory grade on the project, and the rejected woman still hated him.

Now he knew why Howie wanted him here in person. This would be a hard sell and Howie would likely opt for fifteen minutes of accolades for his latest protégé before the personal introduction.

Lee braced himself for what was coming, and then decided to try a different tack. Charge and take the offensive. "Tell me about her, Howie. Is she mature, professional? What has she worked on, lately? How about a clearance?" He fired his questions like bullets from an automatic weapon.

When he paused to reload, Howie cut in. "Whoa, settle down, Lee. Her name is Jennifer Akihara. She just finished her master's program in Computing Security and she's doing research while she waits to start her Ph.D. program."

"So what research is she working on?"

"I'm not authorized to tell you the specifics of her work, but Jennifer has developed network traffic-analysis algorithms, including data mining for suspicious activity on the Internet. Her current work is for the FBI, but she has also worked for NSA. In fact, NSA has a standing job offer for Jennifer whenever she decides she's through being a student. She's the best I've got and you won't find anyone better."

Maybe only one in a thousand graduate students could even attempt such work. Perhaps one in a million grad students possessed an intellect capable of performing it. He took a quick stab at the math. The answer he came up with blew his mind.

"That's impressive. I accept your offer." He heard himself say the words, but Lee still had reservations about allowing a young, immature, female grad student have any involvement in critical issues affecting his work, the well-being of National Aerospace, and possibly his job. This time he might be risking a lot more than a poor grade on his transcript.

Howie cleared his throat. "There's one thing you should keep in mind when working with Jennifer."

Here it comes—Lee Brandt's worst-case scenario—the reason I should have turned Howie down on this offer. He tried to sound nonchalant. "What's that?"

"Don't ever lie to her, Lee. Don't even let it appear that you're trying to deceive her."

Maybe he was being overly paranoid. "I don't intend to lie to her, Howie. But why the warning?"

"Lee, just don't do it, or believe me, you'll be sorry."

The warning was puzzling, but why should he worry? He didn't practice lying and deceit. "Thanks for the tip. How soon can we get started?"

"I'll be right back. She's down the hall in our computer..." Still talking when he walked away, Howie's words trailed off as he scurried down the hall.

****

Jennifer stood in the computer lab reflecting on her appearance. She was short, slender, small, and often mistaken for a teenager despite her intelligence and maturity. Being mistaken for a much younger person really aggravated her. No. Aggravation was a euphemism. She generally flew into a raging tirade.

When some men saw a young, attractive, and rather small woman, they assumed she was naïve and vulnerable. That assumption brought outright evil in the worst of men.

She wished to be taller, stronger, and to look normal. Maybe slightly on the nice side of normal. Were those three wishes or one wish with three parts? Her normally sharp mind seemed a little fuzzy this evening. But so was mathematics, especially at its outermost edges. Fuzzy, philosophical, and fully fascinating. If she could only see a little further out—

She jumped when a hand touched her shoulder. "Oh...Howie—"

"I didn't mean to startle you. Lee is in my office. Let's go hear about the problem at National Aerospace."

She stared at him, deliberately exaggerating the frown on her forehead. "Can I trust him, Howie?"

Howie hesitated.

She glared at him. "You know what I mean. Can I really trust him?"

"I would trust him with my life, Jennifer. In fact...I would even trust him with yours."

She studied his eyes, looking for any darting, twitching, or—gotcha. No eye contact.

His eyes were focused on her chin.

"You've never, ever played matchmaker with me. That's not what this is all about, is it?"

"I just told Lee you were the best person I know to help him. That's what this is all about." Howie nudged her towards the lab door. He also sidestepped her question.

****

Lee tried to prepare for some young, geeky woman who hated liars. He decided to remain seated when she entered. He didn't want to offend the female geek.

When Jennifer Akihara entered the room, some involuntary reflex lifted him to his feet in the presence of the petite, stunning beauty. Long black hair. Large, almond-shaped brown eyes that threatened to suck him in like a black hole from which he could never escape. Her face was far too perfect to be real. There was more—a whole lot more. Things that any red-blooded man couldn't help but notice.

Lee had never seen anyone like Jennifer Akihara in his life. Recovering from his initial shock, the left side of Lee's brain pushed the panic button.

She's beautiful. Too beautiful. You need to run now!

The right side of his brain shortened the reply.

She's beautiful.

Howie, standing behind Jennifer, was grinning from ear to ear as he watched Lee's complete loss of composure. "Lee, this is Jennifer Akihara. Jennifer, meet Lee Brandt, one of the real systems guys at National Aerospace. By the way, Lee is also a meteorologist."

"Mr. Brandt, Dr. Martin says you've been having some stormy weather in your department." Like Mona Lisa, she wore an enigmatic smile.

Based upon his previous bad experience, that smile on that beautiful face had trouble written all over it. But if Jennifer lived up to even half of her billing, Lee needed her help. "As a matter of fact, I was struck by lightning just before I left work."

"That sounds dangerous."

"Not to me, personally. But it was troubling. I need someone who can help me unravel who's doing what, where, when, and with whom over the Internet. There's suspicious software running on a National Aerospace laptop as we speak."

She stared into his eyes. "What you need, Mr. Brandt, happens to be my specialty."

Those eyes—so intense—he was losing focus

again. "Uh...there's also malware, probably a Trojan, involved. I can't find the doggone thing."

"Malware research was my specialty before I moved into Internet communications analysis and forensics."

With her intelligence and looks, is there anything that's not her specialty? She could make winning beauty pageants her specialty, if she wanted to.

Even his left brain agreed with that assessment.

When his gaze refocused, she stood waiting for him to return from his mental excursion. It took some time because he had never seen such a beautiful female, and Jennifer Akihara was indisputably female.

Lee tried to fortify his defenses with logic from the left side of his brain.

Beautiful means she's probably conceited and arrogant. Her initial effects will wear off.

The right side of his brain had a different assessment.

Fat chance!

"So are you in grad school?"

"Technically no. I finished my master's in Computing Security last fall. I'm doing contract research, working with Howie, until I start my Ph.D. program this fall." Her Mona-Lisa smile returned. "Mr. Brandt, I'm sure I can help you."

The subject was...uh...the classified data. It took his brain a few seconds to catch up. "There's some urgency because classified information was compromised."

Come on, man. You know that's not the issue here.

Despite Howie's warning, Lee realized he stood on the threshold of deception before the work with Jennifer even began. He guessed she didn't have a security clearance. If things started going south, he would use the clearance as an excuse to send her back to Howie, though her role wouldn't require access to any restricted data. The consequences of deception Howie warned him about...he might have to live with them.

"That's not a problem. I have a Top Secret SCI clearance. It was required for the work I performed for NSA."

SCI...so she had one of those compartmentalized clearances above Top Secret. So high above that even some of the clearance designations were classified.

Lee was out of excuses. And he was impressed with her qualifications. He was impressed with everything about Ms. Akihara.

Come on, man. You really need to get beyond this mind-numbing reaction to her.

Maybe Howie was right, and Jennifer's involvement would work out fine. Nevertheless, he continued questioning her background. "Top secret and higher clearances aren't given away freely. How did you, as a college student, get NSA to run the clearance for you?"

"Mr. Brandt, it has been my experience that you don't get NSA to run anything. They read a research paper I wrote and came to me because they wanted the two forensic data-analysis algorithms I developed. They planned to use one to analyze web logs while the other analyzed raw network traffic. My algorithms enable them to do the analyses and subsequent correlation of data much faster, and with far less complete data, than the standard techniques."

"How do you use the correlated data?"

"The short and sweet of it is that it helps the authorities find and catch the bad guys without having to process so much data by brute force and without having to use those highly targeted programs. That is…it does when the laws don't stop us cold. Living in a free society is both wonderful and frustrating, depending upon whether you're an ordinary, law-abiding citizen, or one who's tasked with catching those who aren't."

Maybe her answer was a bit condescending, but he had come across as an idiot. He deserved a little condescension.

She was beautiful, intelligent, and self-confident.

He sensed no arrogance.

When she talked about her work, she let it stand on its own merit—no bragging.

It was time for the invitation. "How soon can you come over to my work area at National Aerospace? I need help locating some people…the type who aren't law-abiding citizens."

"I can show up in about thirty minutes. I just need to collect some tools of the trade."

"Sounds good. Do you drive?"

At Lee's question, Jennifer's gaze burned into his eyes like laser beams.

You fool!

The accusation came from Lee's right brain. *You should've asked her if she had a car. Look at her. The DOD could have used those eyes for its missile defense system. If you insult her again, she'll burn a hole right through you.*

Her laser look ended in a frown. "I drive, Mr. Brandt, and I own a car."

He cleared his throat. "You'll need to park outside of the gate in the lot at North Fourth and Park Place. I'll meet you there to get your visitor's badge."

"I'll see you in thirty minutes."

When Jennifer walked out the door, Howie's grin said he was very pleased with himself.

That made Lee nervous. Jennifer Akihara, already distracted and intimidated him...maybe there was something else going on here.

"So what do you think, Lee?" A grin spanned Howie's face. "Her IQ is in the over one-hundred eighty category, maybe as high as two hundred. Very near Einstein's."

Lee turned to leave, not wanting to voice his thoughts.

"I trust you with Jennifer, Lee. She needs someone to..." The door swung and latched, cutting off Howie's last words.

Lee drove back to work, but his thoughts kept returning to the young woman...Jennifer. Part of him wanted to plunge in and drown in the depths of those intense, brown eyes. Another part feared her eyes might burn through him like a cutting torch, leaving a scarred, disfigured heart in the aftermath.

He'd parked his Mustang outside the gate in the public lot. He would have to escort Jennifer to this lot when they finished working. Though he usually opted for a secure parking area inside the compound, Randy Matthews was on duty at the gate shack. He could be trusted to watch out for Lee's classic car.

Lee hurried through the turnstile and the cipher-locked door to his desk. He needed to prepare for Jennifer's visit. First, he compiled a list of known facts about the breach, and then he listed his suspicions. Finally, he made a list of things he still needed to know.

Still needed to know—did that category include more about Jennifer Akihara?

****

As Jennifer collected her DVDs containing the software tools she'd need at National Aerospace, she reflected on Lee Brandt. He was not a typical computer nerd or geek. That had set off all of her alarms at once. He was on the rugged side of handsome. He stood when she entered the room. But his eyes went all gaga when he saw her.

He would probably be like all the others. Howie might think he was a good guy, but she watched his IQ drop to near zero when she walked into the room—a sure sign of trouble.

Jennifer had doubts about spending an evening working with Lee Brandt. But she told Howie she'd give it a shot. She hoped she wouldn't have to give Mr. Brandt one...from her Smith and Wesson.

Speaking of shots...she pulled the gun from her purse and secured it in her locker in the computer lab. She had never been inside the gates at National Aerospace, but she assumed they, like other defense contractors, had policies preventing employees from taking guns through their gates.

Grabbing her pack, she was ready for National Aerospace. But was she ready for Mr. Lee Brandt? It was too bad she couldn't trust men, because there was something about him that—no, there was nothing about Lee Brandt except a concern that she should keep her distance. She would do her work as quickly as possible and leave.

5

When Lee finished his three lists, he glanced at his watch. Thirty minutes since he'd left Howie's office. He hurried to the gate shack.

Randy stood in the doorway staring down the parking lot. "Hey, Randy, have you seen...uh..." Lee paused, searching for appropriate words to describe Jennifer, "...a young lady arrive here looking for me?"

"Do you mean the Miss Universe candidate with long, dark hair and big, brown eyes? The one who asked me where to park?"

"This is about work, Randy. It's not a social visit."

"That's too bad, Lee. But I bet it's going to be a pleasant work session." Randy's grin spanned the width of his face. "On a scale from one to ten, she's a ninety-nine."

He scowled. "Just get me a visitor's badge form."

Jennifer approached the guard shack.

He hurried, trying to expedite the badging process and minimize her exposure to Randy's obnoxious remarks.

"Jennifer, we'll need your signature here, and Randy needs to see your driver's license." Lee positioned the paper on the counter and turned towards Jennifer. "Please keep the badge clipped on after we enter the compound. Since you're a visitor, you'll need to stay with me at all times after we go through the turnstile."

"And you wouldn't want it to be any other way, right, Lee?"

He glared at Randy, but the security guard's smirk remained on his face.

Jennifer shook her head at Randy's comment and then signed the form.

Ignoring Randy, Lee directed her through the turnstile. He punched the code into the lock. After the click he opened the door and they entered the lab starting a chain of events Lee prayed he wouldn't regret.

Once inside, Jennifer stepped in front of Lee cutting him off. When she turned to face him her laser look was back. "About what you said at the gate...because I'm your visitor, you have to escort me everywhere?"

"Is that a problem?"

Jennifer's gaze bored into him. "If anyone tells me that applies to the restrooms I'm out of here."

"No, it most certainly does not."

He tried to imagine what life must be like for her. Her beauty was stunning, but she looked young and vulnerable. Evidently this combination brought her problems. He would try not to add to them.

He walked to Ram's desk and wiggled the mouse attached to the docking station. "This laptop belonged to the contractor who accessed the classified data. I watched port and IP address usage on this machine for several minutes. It communicated with a computer outside of our firewalls. But I couldn't locate any malware, nor could I trace where the communications were going. That's why I need your help."

"I see you're still logged in...as administrator, I assume?"

He nodded.

Jennifer pulled a DVD from her carrying case and started loading software directly onto Ram's laptop— no flash drive.

Several alarms went off inside his head. This could go very badly for him if they were caught. "What are you loading onto my company's machine?"

"Mr. Brandt...you don't want to know."

"What if I do want to know, but just don't want National Aerospace to know?"

"Trust me on this. You don't know the details of what I'm doing and it's best if we keep it that way. It makes you mostly innocent—well...innocent of anything really serious." She flashed him a glance.

Was that a smirk on her face?

"Innocent of what?" He paused, but she ignored his question. "Ms. Akihara, mostly innocent means partly guilty."

For a woman who hated deception she needed to practice what she preached.

Peering over her shoulder questions began loading like cartridges into his mind. When the magazine in his mind filled his mouth started firing. "You're logging directly onto an outside machine. That's not supposed to be possible. How are you getting out? You need an account on our firewall server to do that, unless you're just logging onto a website from a browser."

Jennifer turned towards Lee and exhaled a forceful sigh. Her eyes narrowed, piercing him with their intensity. "Look, Mr. Brandt, it's OK if you want to keep looking over my shoulder. But please be quiet. I need to concentrate."

The left side of his brain screamed into his left frontal lobe. *Unplug the docking station, you fool, before this gets any worse!*

He listened to the right side and did nothing.

Jennifer opened two windows.

Lee guessed they ran the programs she loaded onto the laptop.

One window displayed information on local port usage and the other displayed the output from something running on another computer, one outside National Aerospace.

He couldn't be sure, but the range of IP addresses scrolling across the screen indicated she had access to a network traffic database for a huge chunk of the Internet. Was it NSA's database?

He noticed a third program minimized to the tray at the bottom of the screen. What had he gotten himself into?

She could get them both hung out to dry, first by National Aerospace, and then by the federal government.

After three or four minutes of intense concentration, Jennifer turned. "Well, I found the malware. It was cleverly disguised. I would bet money it's designed to replicate and spread, but I'd have to reverse engineer it to be sure. We don't have time to do that tonight. I captured the file so we can fingerprint the malevolent code."

"Is that what's displayed in the window on the left—the malware information?"

She nodded.

"And the window on the right?"

She squinted and frowned. "That one is going to take a while. It looks like the malware is communicating with an unknown hacker at some unknown location. The problem is he, or she, is hiding behind some compromised machines."

He rubbed his chin and thought about his initial findings. "The compromised machines wouldn't happen to be in Texas and Colorado, would they?"

Jennifer looked up and her eyes widened. "Uh...yes...well, two of them are. We'll get back to that subject in a moment. As I was explaining, my algorithm utilizes a little graph theory along with heuristics derived from Internet-wide communications patterns, to resolve the circuitous path that a line of communication like this one is using."

"Would you please just tell me what it is you actually do to wade through that mess and find the bad guy?"

She smiled.

What would life be like if he woke up every day knowing he would see that smile on that face? He was being ridiculous.

"Mr. Brandt?"

"Uh...yes. We're finding the bad guys."

"And we do that by running my algorithm for Internet-scale analysis using data queried from one of NSA's computers—data that was collected from servers on the backbone of the Internet and some other carefully selected machines." Jennifer swiveled her chair to face him. "We know a lot about both Internet topology and routing. I used that knowledge to reduce the number of servers we need to analyze to detect the bad guys doing their dirty work. I also used it to formulate some heuristics to make the required computation manageable. Mr. Brandt...do you remember those classes of complexity you learned about in theory of computing?"

"Yes. P, NP, NP-Complete, recursively

unsolvable—I dreaded that subject coming up during my master's oral exam."

"Well, identifying heuristics that can turn some of those seemingly intractable problems into computable ones, and implementing algorithms to do so, is my specialty."

Clearly Jennifer was working at the fringes of mathematics and computer science, pushing the limits of human knowledge. She intimidated him, but she also strongly attracted him. That intimidated him even further. "OK, assuming you and your tools do all of that, how long do we have to wait to determine where this guy is located?"

"With this algorithm and this scale of analysis, there's no way to predict how long it will take. It may be five minutes, and then again, it may be five hours or more."

He gestured towards the lab door. "Well then, shall we make a run to a coffee house, or grab something to eat while we wait?"

"Uh...just a minute. The intermediate printout I directed to standard output indicates we're converging quickly to a solution. I think this run is of the five-minute variety. Let me look at what's coming back to the screen for a minute. Maybe we've found the bad guys."

"Sounds good to me." Although going to get coffee with Jennifer sounded better.

Jennifer sat silently until more text appeared in the window she monitored. "Mr. Brandt, what software does your company use for its VPN?"

"Please, just call me Lee."

She continued watching text scroll through the window on the laptop. "OK...Lee, what sof—

rather...what protocol does your VPN client use on the company laptops?"

He noticed she didn't reciprocate with an invitation to use her first name.

"The VPN clients all use IPSec."

"That's what I thought you were going to say."

"Is that a problem?"

"No. But I think these guys hacked your VPN client and hijacked it."

Lee gestured with his right hand, fingers spread wide. "They hijacked the software every National Aerospace employee uses for telecommuting?"

"Evidently. And that's going to cause National Aerospace a lot of problems, especially if the bad guys start grabbing account information from infected machines."

He didn't like where this was leading. "So now I suppose you're going to tell me a hacker can actually look like one of our employees working from home, yet be at another location and have control of an infected PC located inside the company?"

"That's exactly what I'm telling you. You could have a botnet inside your firewall. Or if they know precisely what they want they can just access it like an employee would."

"Wonderful."

This was a whole lot more than Ram looking at one classified drawing. The military side of National Aerospace had developed dozens of weapons and surveillance systems that could all be compromised by a scheme to access the classified engineering data from DEDS. The commercial side had trade secrets, proprietary information, and employee identity data.

Lee could certainly say "I told you so" to Barry

and their CEO, but that would give him little satisfaction, because Jennifer's discovery transcended his worst fears by an order of magnitude.

She pointed to the laptop screen. "They can communicate right through your firewall for quite a while before you discover what's happening. By then, they will likely have obtained what they're looking for and will split, covering their tracks as they go."

Lee stared at the wall. The national security ramifications were frightening to him. "And from where is our friendly hacker controlling this machine?"

"He will appear to be local." Jennifer sighed sharply. "But to answer your question, it's more than one place. Probably more than one hacker. Who knows how many infected machines there are in this building, or elsewhere inside National Aerospace. That's the good news."

"Great." He rolled his eyes. "What's the bad news?"

"I can sum it up in four words...Iran, Yemen, Colombia, Mexico." She studied him as she spoke.

"Not good. Not good at all," he muttered. "I've heard Iran has been increasing its presence in Latin America and that it funds the recruiting and training of terrorists there. Do you think we've encountered an instance of Iran's activity a little closer to home?"

Jennifer paused for a moment, squinting and playing with the ends of her hair. "Perhaps...but we've still got the Yemen factor to consider. Some U.S. based companies used technology training in Yemen to try to ameliorate the situation. You know...give the guys a good career and they'll love us. The jury's still out on its effectiveness. But there could be a cause-and-effect relationship between the technology training and the sophisticated hacking we uncovered."

"I see the logic. It could account for both the Trojan and the hacked VPN clients."

"But Mexico…" Jennifer paused, fiddling with her hair again. "Seeing activity in Mexico really bothers me, especially after the recent increase in alliances between drug cartels and Islamic terrorists."

That was news to him. "I know Mexico is littered with drug cartels, but who reported their cooperation with Islamic terrorists?"

She studied him again. "General Pace testified to Congress about this trend a few years ago. At the time, the activity was confined to South America. More recently, a Navy admiral reiterated General Pace's concerns saying the activity was moving north."

He could sure conjure up some frightening possibilities from Jennifer's discoveries. "So what was the congressional reaction to the warning—the more recent one?"

She exhaled sharply. "Basically…our politicians either pooh-poohed it, or shrugged."

"That's all?" Lee frowned and gave her a palms-up shrug. "Not even any saber-rattling?"

"That's it." Jennifer sighed. "Even after we exposed the link between Iran and Hezbollah in Latin America."

"That link sounds like it might explain what we saw tonight, especially if the cooperation has extended northward into Mexico."

The look in her eyes became intense. "Explain it by which, the military's warning, or the politicians' shrugs?" She was testing the political waters.

It was good to see they were on the same page. The left side of Lee's brain jumped all over his deduction.

Why does that even matter?

When the schizophrenic conversation in his mind ended, he answered her question. "I'd say by both the warnings and the shrugs. But I hate to think about the implications for the USA. Mexico is pretty close to home and the border is open to anyone who has a will to cross it."

"I don't think Mexico will do much to remedy that problem. Intelligence shows the cartels bought off the police and many government officials. Or assassinated them as examples. The drug cartels are in control across much of Mexico and they're recruiting gangs on our side of the border. In addition, we've observed them trafficking not only drugs, but also people, chemical, and biological warfare materials, and now we've even detected the movement of some nuclear materials."

"Nuclear materials?"

What were her sources of information? It was probably best not to ask. "Wow. Mix that stuff with terrorists and you've got—"

"Maybe Uncle Sam's funeral if we don't wake up and act now. Lee, we don't know what part of all that we stumbled onto tonight. This needs a lot more analysis, so we've got to report our findings to DHS, the FBI, NSA—"

"And we need to pray somebody listens, connects the dots, and is willing to take action." He stared at the compromised laptop.

Jennifer shrugged. "You can pray if you want to, but I don't put much stock in that sort of thing. I'm more into doing it myself."

A shrug—do it myself—doesn't pray. Either she's been

burned by some church, or she's an honest-to-goodness agnostic.

If the opportunity arose he would ask her a few questions about her views. The left side of his brain repeated its previous question.

Why does it matter to you?

The right side threw a right cross to the jaw. It KO'd the left side. The fight was over. There would be ramifications, but he shoved that thought from his mind.

"I think it's time for me to call Joe Morrison at Computing Security. He's a good starting point. Joe has contacts within the FBI, DHS, and the police departments. He's part of the Metropolitan Area JTTF. You know, the Joint Terrorism Task Force."

"Sounds good." Jennifer positioned her hands on the laptop keyboard. "And while you're calling him I'm going to eliminate this little Trojan. Then I think I'll call my contact at NSA."

"Yes. Please eliminate it. Now, let's see...the FBI, DHS, NSA, and Computing Security—that should just about cover the bases." He dialed Joe Morrison's Computing Security cell-phone number. Joe would respond to a call on that phone anywhere, anytime.

"Joe Morrison here."

"Joe, it's Lee. I'm at work and I've got some bad news. I need to tell you this in person."

"Is it that serious?"

"I'm afraid so. Are you at home?"

"Yes. Why don't you come over? We can meet in my study."

"I'm on my way."

Jennifer continued talking to someone at NSA. A few seconds later, she hung up and sat for a moment, staring across the room.

"I told Joe there was some bad news I needed to tell him in person," Lee said. "I haven't told him about your role yet, but I need you to explain what you found. You'll be a lot more convincing than me."

She squinted and frowned. "Since Joe doesn't know about me yet, he could—"

"Completely flip out and have us both locked up."

Jennifer straightened in her chair. "Wonderful. You *will* tell him you brought me in on this and that I *am* cleared for any level of information we might be dealing with?"

Lee noted the change in her posture. Though they hadn't dealt with any classified data he should have anticipated her response. "Locked up" could end her career.

"Of course I will. And Joe's a sensible guy. Officially, he'll chew me out. But unofficially he'll be tickled pink that I brought you in. If anyone gives us any flak you can count on me to take whatever blame they throw our way."

"I guess I have to, don't I?"

"Have to what?"

"Count on you." Jennifer stared into his eyes.

Her penetrating gaze turned his brain inside out.

He looked away. He was mentally and emotionally exposed to her, including the thoughts coming from the right side of his brain.

Jennifer was far more than a pretty face. She was incredible in every sense of the word and he was drawn to her by a magnetic force so powerful it scared him. He hadn't a clue where all this would lead—the security breach, the investigation, Jennifer—any of it.

6

Lee escorted Jennifer out of the compound and walked past the gate shack. No Randy. Good. He wouldn't have to expose Jennifer to more suggestive remarks.

When they entered the north end of the parking area he glanced at her. "You can follow me over to Joe's place. It's just about a mile east of here, a block off from North Fourth Avenue."

"OK. When you tell Joe I'm involved in the investigation..."

"Don't worry about Joe. I can handle him." A short way down the lot he stopped, smiled, and gestured to their left. "There's my car."

Jennifer pivoted towards his car and stopped. Her eyes lit up and checked out his Mustang like a scanner digitizing an image. She smiled warmly at him. "A classic. Very nice, Lee."

It was the second genuine smile she'd shown him. What that smile did for an already beautiful face was incredible.

Good taste in cars. I wonder about her taste in men.

No, I don't wonder anything about her.

Now in control, the right side of his brain turned a deaf ear and continued to savor the smile.

"I'll swing by your parking spot and lead you to a shortcut through a couple adjacent lots. And about National Aerospace Computing Security...have no fear, Lee is here."

Even in the dimly-lit parking lot he could see the rolling eyes. She strode down the lot towards her car.

In her presence he couldn't turn a decent phrase. But he sure could turn a decent phrase into something stupid. He pulled out his keys, stopped, and snapped his fingers.

Jennifer's visitor's badge.

Randy wasn't in the gate shack and he forgot to return her badge. When he glanced down the lot Jennifer was nearly to her car. He trotted towards her. "Hey, Ms. Akihara...Jennifer. I forgot—"

The area lit up like mid-day. A deafening boom sounded behind him. The shock wave blindsided him with the force of an NFL linebacker, knocking him forward to the concrete. He stuck out his arm to protect his face. His body rode on his right forearm for several feet, while the rough concrete rasped off his coat sleeve and much of the skin underneath it.

He lay sprawled out on the parking lot pavement. His mind struggled to comprehend what had happened. When he picked himself up, he shook his head to remove the cobwebs. There were too many of them. Blood ran down his right forearm. Pain brushed some of the cobwebs away.

Explosion.

Arm burning and ears ringing, he looked for the source of the blast. It came from what had been his car—from what was now only a blackened shell. The sense of loss hit him in his gut. He might never be able to replace that car. He brushed away a few more cobwebs. The clearing of his mind brought a bigger worry. *Better a bombed car than a bombed body.* But the bombing attempt had failed, so...

The air emptied from his lungs and he drew a deep breath. His pulse quickened. The realization hit him like a stinging slap on the face. They were in big trouble, but the incoming flak wouldn't be the kind that got one fired. It would be the kind that got fired at one—bullets from people who killed to keep secrets.

Despite their delicate search on the infected computer their foray must've triggered attention and it wasn't all coming from some hacker halfway around the world.

Jennifer stood motionless by her car staring across the parking lot at the blackened remains of Lee's Mustang.

He sprinted towards her. "Jennifer, start your car, now!"

She jumped towards her car door, eyes wide with fear.

A staccato stream of gunshots sounded from near the gate shack as Lee slid into her sedan.

A large, black SUV turned from the street. It sped past the gate shack and into the parking lot. The headlights swung in an arc, the light beams stopping on Jennifer's car. The SUV rolled down the lot towards them.

He fought to control his racing thoughts. "Go, go, go! Turn left into the next lot and floor it straight through to the street."

"Are you sure it's us they're after?" Her voice shook.

"Shall we stop and ask them, Jenn?"

Jennifer jerked towards him, mouth open and frowning.

What did I say?

This wasn't the time to analyze her response.

"We've got to make it to the police station."

Her head jerked around again. Why was she looking at him?

"Watch where you're going. They're coming, that black SUV." Lee rolled down his fogged window. "They shot at Randy and they weren't using a single-shot .22."

In a road race, her small sedan would be no match for the powerful SUV.

She said nothing, hands gripping the steering wheel as she focused on driving.

"Just do whatever you have to do to keep them from closing on. us. I'm calling 911, now." Lee reached for his cell phone.

"What's the best way to the police station?" Her voice was stronger, as if she'd come to grips with what was happening,

Gutsy woman. Good. Because their survival depended on her.

"Turn right onto North Park. Keep going south. You'll come to it."

He stuck his head out the window and looked at the headlights behind them.

The SUV angled straight across the parking lot. Its driver ignored the rows, sidewalks, everything. The gunmen would overtake them in a few seconds. The bright headlights vibrated as the vehicle bounced over all of the concrete curbs and parking space dividers in its path. Their pursuer's two-fold intent became clear.

Keep them from heading south towards the police and get within easy firing range.

If they turned south their pursuers might cut behind the building, cut them off on Park, then cut them down with their weapons. "Turn left. Get behind that building. Then left on North Park."

She flashed him a glance and another frown. "What? Away from the police station?"

"If you wanna stay alive do it."

Jennifer yanked the wheel to the left.

Lee's body slammed against the side of the car.

Their pursuers whipped around accelerating to intercept them before Jennifer could put the building between them. Two guns jutted through the windows of the SUV and swung towards them.

"They're gonna shoot! Get around the building."

Jennifer responded quickly despite her panic, accelerating across the next parking lot and pressing Lee back in the seat.

But the headlights behind them loomed too close.

Gripping the arm rest he thumbed his cell phone open. "Go Jenn! Get—"

Bullets sprayed from an automatic weapon shattering the top of the sedan's rear window.

Like buckshot fragments of glass pelted Lee's head and left hand. His cell phone flew from his fingers. Blood trickled down the back of his neck and his hand, while his cell phone danced on top of the dash.

His hand throbbed. He swept his right hand across the dashboard attempting a backhand catch of the phone before it bounced out of reach.

Jennifer clipped a curb. The sharp bump launched the cell phone up.

Lee tried to catch it in midair. It bounced off the heel of his hand. His hopes of reaching a 911 operator flew out the window with his cell phone.

Jennifer rounded the building acquiring a temporary shield from the gunfire. She flashed him a wide-eyed glance. "Lee, are you OK?"

"I think so."

Lee checked his wounds. No pain from his head. He ran his fingers through his hair. They came away bloody. *Only a scalp wound. A lot of blood, but no serious damage.* Blood trickled from several cuts on his hand, but he could move his fingers.

They passed beyond the building and approached North Park Street.

"Now which way?"

"Go left. Then just do whatever you have to do to lose them."

"Away from the police station? Are you sure?"

"Yes. Just don't give them any clear shots."

She repositioned her hands on the wheel. "OK, but hang on. No telling what I'll need to do."

She floored it and the car's wheels squealed as they turned left onto North Park. Two wheels caught air when Jennifer took the next left. She yanked the wheel right and they roared through a narrow alleyway.

Smart woman. That big SUV may not fit.

When they turned left to exit the alley the car slid sideways the full width of the street and bumped the curb.

He expected a flat tire, but they rolled along smoothly as they headed west on North Eighth towards the freeway.

Lee stuck his head out and looked behind. He blew the air from his lungs, and then tried to take a calming breath. "I don't see any headlights."

Jennifer replicated his breathing exercise. "Maybe we lost them." She glanced his way. "You're bleeding."

"It's nothing. Just cuts from the glass."

"There's a pack of tissues in the glove box."

"Thanks, but I'd rather have a cell phone. Do you have one with you?"

"No. I left my phone and...well, some other things at the computer lab before I drove over to National Aerospace. Didn't know what I could take through your security. And Lee...I'll bet you don't play shortstop, do you?"

Lee studied her face. Sarcastic or...he couldn't tell. "No, I pitch."

"Sorry about the bad hop I gave you—you know, just before it went out the window. Do you think we lost them?"

"Maybe, but I'd recommend you just keep it floored as much as possible. We've got to make sure they can't find us."

"We're on city streets. I'll do my best. But what about the police station?"

He looked down the street. "Let's get further west before we turn south and work our way back. Make sure you avoid the freeway. They could run us down easily there. No place to hide."

Jennifer turned left onto a small street. They headed south on the frontage road towards the police station. She glanced at him again. "I'm going to slow down so we blend in more with the other traffic."

A couple of blocks ahead, a large vehicle closed quickly on them.

Unfortunately, their proximity to the freeway left only one southbound street available to Jennifer. He wasn't the only one who had realized that.

He squeezed hard on the armrest. "It's them."

Jennifer jerked the wheel right and veered onto a small street terminating in a T at its west end.

He could see the freeway's supporting structures

straight ahead.

At the T she turned left and mashed the accelerator.

Their pursuers again appeared one block ahead of them. Now they had only one option.

Lee gasped as Jennifer took it. She ran a stop sign and steered to the right onto a ramp that placed them southbound on the interstate.

"They will—" When he glanced at her face he closed the spigot of words he intended to spew.

The wet tracks on her cheek glistened under a freeway light.

This woman was doing her best—far better than he could have done. A strong urge to hold and comfort her replaced his unspoken, harsh words.

She accelerated to well above the speed limit, but the SUV's now familiar headlights shot down the ramp and closed on them. The gunmen had them where they wanted them—a place with no shelter from bullets.

Her intense stare down the road indicated a desperate search to keep them out of gunshot range until they could exit if they ever got the chance.

He tried to think of some way to escape. His mind only drew blanks. Lee looked ahead at three semis rolling along as a convoy in the second lane from the right on this four-lane section of southbound I-5.

When they approached the trucks Jennifer slowed.

"What are you doing?"

"Heading for cover. You'd better pray this works, Lee, or else I—" She didn't finish.

Lee, lowered his head and fired a silent prayer to the only One he believed could protect them in a situation so out of control and desperate.

When Jennifer pulled even with the left side of the

rearmost semi's cab, the big SUV closed to within shooting range. Jennifer looked towards the cab of the semi, and then at Lee. "I hope you pray better than you handle a cell phone, because here we go."

"Jennifer, I don't think—" The staccato popping of automatic weapons fire truncated Lee's words.

Jennifer jerked the wheel to the right as bullets ripped through the rear of her car. Amid horns blaring and air brakes hissing they shot the gap and emerged in the far right lane.

Lee scanned a full circle around them.

She was incredible. Her move had saved their lives.

He appended admiration to the growing list of qualities that attracted him.

"You OK, Jenn?"

"I think so. That truck driver seemed to get the picture. He slowed, and then closed the gap behind us. My compliments on your prayer, Lee."

"Don't thank me. I should be thanking you. But I hope those goons don't get mad and fire at the trucker. On the other hand, that might get them squashed by a semi."

"Are there any exits near here?"

"Not sure—don't think so—not for a couple of miles, anyway." He turned to survey the car for critical damage. He saw none, but a vehicle slowed, trying to swing in behind the trucks.

Two cars impeded the gunmen's vehicle, but they would soon be on the sedan's tail.

If Jennifer couldn't concoct some evasive maneuver they would be trapped in the right lane by the semis on their left and the slow driver ahead of them.

"They're right behind us."

Jennifer accelerated. Was she going to try passing the slow car on the right shoulder? Her car was small, but it wouldn't fit between the car and the concrete barrier on the right.

"Jenn, you can't—" Lee held his breath as Jennifer maneuvered between the car and the barrier. He leaned hard to his left when sparks flew from the passenger-side mirror as it scraped the concrete, and then he gasped for air after they shot through unscathed.

He stared, wondering about her sanity.

She glanced at him. "I don't know how much longer I can hold them off. Since you believe in prayer, I would suggest you do that now."

"I have been. We're still safe, aren't we?" Lee said the words, but he felt anything but safe.

The concrete barrier ended.

Behind them, the SUV forced the slow driver onto the shoulder and surged within shooting distance.

"Here they come." His voice grew soft, resigned. "I don't know what we can do about it this time."

Jennifer clenched her jaw. "Maybe we...you'd better pray this works, because there's nothing else to try."

She jerked the wheel to the left. Red lights flashed on the back of the semi's cab.

Can't she see the gap's too small?

Lee tucked his head and braced for the collision.

Then came...no contact...nothing.

Lee lifted his head.

They were in the lane to the left of the trucks.

He watched the truckers close ranks, leaving the SUV trapped in the rightmost lane with cars now blocking both ahead and behind.

When he looked over at Jennifer she sat rigid, hands clamped to the wheel, breathing hard.

As he looked beyond her a familiar picture flashed through his mind. "There's a left-lane exit coming up immediately. Take it!"

Jennifer's hands became a blur of motion as she fought to make the off ramp on their left.

The car leaned to the right, as screeching tires and the smell of burnt rubber announced their entrance into the sharp left turn of the ramp. They slid sideways well into the turn, and then she punched the gas pedal. Wheels spinning, they rocketed out of the turn and ran the stop sign at the ramp's end. The sedan fishtailed across the frontage road as Jennifer fought for control after over-steering. They ended up in the left lane of the highway, but she accelerated, angling back into the right.

When Lee regained his bearings, they were westbound on Highway 159. This highway headed into a rural area—an area of forests, mountains, and many small roads. This was Lee's childhood stomping grounds. Surely he could find a way to hide them, or to get help, before the black SUV could backtrack from the next freeway exit.

But there were no phones for miles.

7

Lee watched the needle on the speedometer for a few seconds. It remained above seventy miles per hour. After exiting I-5 in race-car driver fashion, Jennifer drove away from the interstate on Highway 159. Her quick exit bought at least fifteen minutes.

By that time, they would be well on their way to the Kerbyville police station. If the gunmen found them, he and Jennifer would hide, because there were no sure places to reach a phone.

"That last time we cut between the two semis..." Jennifer's voice interrupted his thoughts.

"Yeah?"

"We got through—*between*—them. But...I don't see how. There wasn't enough room. I turned in front of the truck because I had no other choice. Did you pray...or something?"

"It was more like 'or something.'"

"What do you mean?"

"I think I screamed out a prayer about that time."

"I didn't hear you scream."

"That's because it was a silent prayer."

"Well, I'm sure glad you screamed that silent prayer, because I turned into the right front fender of the truck. We should have been full of holes by now...or part of the semi's grill."

"We could still end up full of holes if we can't get to Kerbyville or, failing that, find a good hiding place.

But prayer isn't magic. It depends entirely on the One to Whom we pray."

"I've got some questions about that 'to Whom we pray' part—maybe for later...assuming there is a later." Her voice sounded different, softer. "But right now, what should we do?"

He stared out his window and rubbed his chin. "We need to change directions before they locate us. You'll see a small county road in less than a mile. Turn left onto it, cut your lights, and...please slow down until your eyes adjust. You should be able to drive without the headlights advertising where we are."

Her alto voice went soprano. "But how can I—"

"Don't worry. Your eyes will adjust in a minute or two. When you can see well enough speed up to a comfortable pace. The road is straight for a few miles, until we reach the mountains. We'll do fine without lights as long as a deer doesn't jump in front of us."

"You seem to know this area well. But you didn't really drive around here without your headlights, did you?"

"Oh, yeah. Uh...no. I mean yes, I do know this area well. But my buddies and I only drove without our headlights to—well...only when we needed to."

Jennifer eyed him like his grandmother used to after he'd admitted to some childhood atrocity.

He cleared his throat. "This is where my best friend and I raised Cain while we were growing—"

"I don't doubt that."

Was that a smirk or a smile?

"I hiked, hunted, and fished just about everywhere within thirty miles of here. There's the road. Go left."

Jennifer turned onto the county road and cut the headlights.

Lee's loud sigh came as an echo to Jennifer's. Was the worst over? He prayed it was.

Jennifer stared down the moonlit road ahead of them. "Lee, this is your domain. What do we do now?"

"If no headlights appear we can take this road all the way to Kerbyville. Their police force is small, but it's a good group of guys. I know a couple of them. They'll help us. But we—"

"I don't like buts, Lee." She cut in. "They always seem to introduce something very unpleasant."

"I know, but...uh...however, we still need a contingency plan...just in case those goons stumble across our trail."

"So what do you propose if we can't make it to Kerbyville?"

"There are several roads leading up into the hills. There are places up there where no one could possibly find us. Hiding will buy us time to get help, or time for help to get to us. After my call to Joe and the car bomb, someone should be looking for us. But—"

Jennifer's head jerked around towards him.

"Jenn, this is a necessary 'but.' If we see anyone behind us, even in the far distance, we have to assume it's the goons. In that event we'll take the next road left into the hills."

With the headlights off the instrument-panel lights brightened to daytime intensity. They lit Jennifer's squinting frown.

"Next question...I haven't had any time to think about this until now, but how do you suppose they got to us so quickly? One minute we discovered the hacker's locations, the next they bombed your car."

"You removed the Trojan and ended its transmissions, right?"

"Yes, I did that a few minutes before we left. That stopped the communications. Also, my software pinged the actual machines the hackers used. Let's see...that was maybe twenty minutes or so before I removed the Trojan. They could have detected both events. But I still don't understand how they got to us so quickly."

"I'm guessing Ram had some local contacts, in addition to the remote hackers. If they could communicate in near real time it would account for their quick retaliation. Either Ram is still here, or before he left, he warned his friends at the local goon club to watch out for signs they had been detected and told them how to handle any threats to their investment."

"So we were a threat?" Jennifer voice softened. "I don't feel like a threat."

"Yes, I guess so...rather, I was. Ram knew I would be involved in any investigation of security breaches in our development environment. He counted on me focusing on the classified data. When we went farther than that..." He stuck his index finger into his chest. "...I became their target. I parked my car near the bushes on the east side of the parking area. They could have gotten to my car without Randy spotting them. But they didn't know about your involvement until I ran to your car in the parking lot. That's a good thing, or your car might have been blown up, too. But I'm sorry to have gotten you involved in this, Jenn."

"If I hadn't gotten involved everything would have been just fine, wouldn't it?" She spat the words at him. "They wouldn't have detected our discovery of their plot, so no bombs, no guns, and no danger for either one of us." Her voice crescendoed. "But National Aerospace computers would have remained compromised. The only other scenario that keeps me in the clear is you get blown up in your car and their plot is successful." She paused. "Now which scenario do you prefer, Lee?" The look she flashed him cut like a knife, giving a whole new meaning to looking daggers. Her logic was impeccable, but all that emotion—where did it come from?

"You made your point, Ms. Akihara."

The frown lines disappeared. Her voice grew soft. "So, it's back to Ms. Akihara, now?" Did her voice just quiver?

Distracted by Jennifer's emotions he ignored the question. Though she was still a mystery to him he preferred Jenn, the person, even though the left side of his brain tried to give him logical reasons why he shouldn't. He feared he was beyond reason now.

"Jenn,"—he made a point of saying her first name—"the problem is we know enough to expose much of their organization, the drug cartels, as well as the terrorists. I'm certain Ram was one of the terrorists. Their local contingent needs to respond quickly and they will err on the side of overkill."

"Overkill?" Her voice grew loud again. "Is that possible? Isn't just kill enough?"

"I doubt it. If they don't deal with us before we contact the police they have to start their plotting all over again from square one, from some other place, and with a whole new approach. With what's at stake they won't give up the chase."

"What's at stake..." She paused. "All those weapons systems National Aerospace makes. They could potentially compromise all of them making the U.S. vulnerable to..." She shook her head as she stared down the road. "No. I don't suppose they'll give up.

And being the good terrorists they are, they have guns, explosives, and who knows what else."

"And in my humble opinion, we've seen and heard far too much of guns and bombs tonight."

"More than enough for a lifetime, as far as I'm concerned." Her voice softened again. "Are you hurt, Lee? After the explosion, and then getting hit with glass when they shot out the back window and the second round of shooting…are you really OK?"

He worked the fingers on his left hand. "My left hand throbs a little, but no bullets hit it. I've got a nasty abrasion on my right arm from the explosion knocking me down. But all things considered I'm in pretty good shape."

The dashboard lights illuminated Jennifer's wrinkled nose as she looked at his head. "Did anyone ever tell you you're a redneck?"

"That's the last thing anyone would call me. What do you mean?" He chuckled and put his hand where she was staring. The back of his neck felt rough. "Is that really—"

"Yes, Lee, blood. And it's pretty gross."

"I guess I am a red neck. The shrapnel from those shots into your car's back window sprayed the back of my head. Scalp cuts bleed a lot even when they're small. You know what happened when I was a kid? I cut my head wide open on—"

"I would prefer not to hear about it."

"It's your loss," he quipped. "What about your car? Do the gauges indicate any problems with the fuel, the engine, or anything else?"

Jennifer scanned the dashboard instruments. "The car looks fine best I can tell. But I was worried they might hit a tire or—"

"Or us, maybe?"

"That too, but evidently you screamed at God and got His attention."

"Maybe. But I prefer to think of it as God having some unfulfilled plans for us. Maybe He thinks we both need some more time on planet Earth."

"That's an interesting thought. Why do you suppose He wants us to have more time? To expose the plot?"

He had another hypothesis to offer, but it was too soon to test it. "Maybe...or perhaps you and I—Jennifer?"

Her eyes widened. "What is it?"

A light flashed in the periphery of his vision. He turned and stared behind them. "Have you been hitting the brakes in the turns?"

Jennifer pounded her forehead with her palm. "Stupid, stupid. How could I have done that?"

"It's OK. I didn't think about it, either, but the car that just turned onto the county road behind us may have. We have to assume it's them."

"So, country boy, what does the contingency plan look like from here?"

"Why don't you slow a little without hitting the brakes and then slip your transmission into low. That will slow us down further. Turn left onto the dirt road that's coming up in a few seconds. If we had our choice of roads to take this is the best one we could choose."

"Are you just trying to make me feel better about advertising where we are?"

"No, Jenn."

"So, it's Jenn again?" Despite their precarious situation, Jennifer flashed him a smile.

He ignored the question. But, Jennifer herself—she

was impossible to ignore despite the danger. Neither did he ignore her smile when he addressed her informally. She was right. He did want her to feel better—to feel good. But more importantly, he wanted to keep her alive.

"Jenn ...you didn't blow it tonight. What you did behind the wheel was amazing and you did it with our lives hanging in the balance. Not once, but over and over again. Holten Creek Road is the best road for us tonight because it leads to the best place to hide. You'll see. Now let's roll along slowly and hope they don't turn in behind us."

She rolled onto Holten Creek Road.

In silence they scrutinized the county lane behind them.

"Look, Lee. They're going by."

"They are. But they slowed as they passed the road."

Jennifer's frown returned. "Without me pushing on the brakes there's no way they could have seen us is there?"

"Only if we kicked up some dust when we turned in and their lights happened to pick it up. They're probably just slowing at every crossroad to take a look. Why don't you roll up to the top of the next hill and try to stop with—"

"I know, without using the brakes."

Lee twisted in his seat to look behind them. "We'll be able to see all the way back to the county road from up there. Let's wait on the hill and if they don't show up any time soon it means they drove over the mountain. With them on the other side we can turn around and take an alternate route to Kerbyville."

"How long do you think we should wait?"

"Not more than thirty minutes. More than that and the pre-dawn twilight will make us too visible en route to Kerbyville, especially if they stop on the pass and use it as a lookout."

"Lee..." Jennifer paused.

"Yes?"

"I've been wondering about what you said—that maybe God had a purpose for us surviving tonight—something left for us to do."

"And what do you think about that idea?"

"In my job I've noticed how easily I get bogged down in the details of network traffic analysis—so bogged down I sometimes miss the big picture—the really important thing I'd never want to miss. Maybe it happens in life as a whole."

At this awkward juncture, was God opening a door?

Lee shot a prayer-arrow heavenward and stepped into the opening. "I know what you mean. It does seem to happen in life, too. I've just forgotten about God at times, because of all the distracting details of life."

Jennifer twisted in her seat to face him. "Why do you suppose that, almost instinctively, we start calling out to Him when serious trouble comes? It's almost like we evolved that way for self-preservation."

"Wouldn't that be survival of the fit-less? What I mean is...calling out to a non-existent being for help wouldn't do much to preserve us. I think a personal God wants to have a relationship with the people He made. Perhaps He uses danger, or other attention-grabbing events, to start the conversation."

"Maybe. But many people, like the goons chasing us, aren't good. They are the epitome of evil. Why would God want to have a relationship with anyone evil?"

God had swung the door wide open.

They needed to wait here for a few minutes more to allow the gunmen to cross the small mountain range on the county road. In case the goons turned around at the base of the mountains, Lee kept an eye on the road behind them while he continued the discussion. "I can't completely answer that question. But if we're honest with ourselves there's some amount of evil in all of us. We've all lied, cheated, and perhaps stolen at some time. God would need to create a plan to reconcile relationships with people who just don't measure up to the standards for a relationship with a good God. Reconciling the relationship between a good God and imperfect people is the very heart of Christianity."

Jennifer glanced at the gear shift handle. Her finger traced its contours. "But the amount of evil in the world still bothers me. Why would a good God even allow it to exist? It's hard for me to believe God created the terrorists who are chasing us."

He watched her nervous finger. "God didn't create terrorists. He created people. Some, like Ram, of their own free will, have chosen to be terrorists. We can't pin the blame on God."

She looked down again and her frown returned. "That's logical...I guess. But evil people like the gunmen chasing us just seem to contradict the existence of a good God."

"I agree, unless you first understand love."

Jennifer looked into his eyes again.

"Think about it this way, Jenn. If God wants a loving relationship with people, how love-based would it be if people had no choice—if they were just forced to love God? I mean, if you were God and you wanted me to have a loving relationship with you, you would have to give me the freedom to choose you, or reject you, right?"

Jennifer opened her mouth to speak, but quickly closed it. She looked down at the gear shift and her eyes narrowed. The frown faded as she raised her head. They each peered into the other's eyes for a moment, and then Jennifer averted her gaze.

Trying to decipher her reactions, he first thought Jennifer realized she had never personally chosen God. Then he became concerned he had chosen unwisely by making the analogy personal between the two of them. While he vacillated between his two takes on her response a third thought came to mind.

They were being followed again. A car just turned onto the dirt road and moved slowly their way.

Jennifer must have seen it too, because she hit the ignition before he could speak. "What now, Lee? This is *your* old stomping grounds."

He locked his gaze on the approaching vehicle. "They're moving slowly. Let's do the same. Keep your speed under fifteen miles-per-hour and—"

"I know. Don't use the brakes."

They rolled down the backside of the hill. Despite the lurking danger Lee was surprised his mind seemed focused and sharp. Thankful for the moment of clarity he planned their escape.

Rubbing his chin he tried to recall the distance from the hill to the base of the mountain directly below the mountaintop spire—the mountaintop he'd played on countless times as a kid. It was about one-half mile.

They were one mile in on Holten Creek Road. If the gunmen drove towards them at twenty miles-per-hour he and Jennifer would reach the spot below the spire with a three-minute lead. In three minutes he could put nearly four hundred yards between them and the goons. In the big Douglas fir trees on the mountainside that distance should provide protection from gunfire.

Four hundred yards.

It would have to be enough.

"Jenn, speed up a little. When I say stop, hit the brakes, cut the engine, then slide over and get out on my side. Try not to leave obvious footprints showing where we're going. We'll be running off to my side of the road through some bushes."

"When is this all going to happen?"

"In about forty-five seconds. Just remember this. If they were going to find us this was the best place for us to be in the entire county, except perhaps the Kerbyville Police Station."

"I think you're an incurable optimist, Lee Brandt."

"Maybe...but see the big tree on the right?"

"I see it. Is that where we stop?"

"Yes. Crank the wheel to the right and try to block the road with your car. It might make them think we went up the road on foot, but we're going up the mountain, instead. Do it now."

8

8:00 a.m., March 18th

Lee led Jennifer from the car nearly two hours ago and somehow had kept them both alive through the physically and emotionally exhausting climb up the mountain. Emotionally exhausting...that was an understatement. The gunmen's bullets had nearly grazed Jennifer's legs.

The sun was well above the horizon, now. Filtered by tree branches it provided some badly needed warmth. A night without sleep and slowing after the long climb left him chilled and fatigued.

Jennifer must be on her last legs.

At least she still has legs.

The sun also provided good visibility for the gunmen.

Lee planned to remedy that in a few minutes. He led Jennifer southward along the mountain slope near the base of the limestone spire. When they reached the second limestone outcropping, Lee studied the caves above them. There were several. That fact alone should confuse and delay the men chasing them.

He hoped they'd search the large cave first. If so, they might never come out.

He chuckled.

Jennifer raised her gaze from the rocky ground to his face. "What's so funny about a bunch of cold, dark holes in a limestone rock? Please enlighten me?"

Despite their situation it was easy to grin whenever he looked at her. "I was just thinking about the big cave at the base of the rock," he whispered. "That's the first cave most people would pick to look in. If they go in there looking for us they'll be bat fodder before they ever find their way out."

She followed and worked her way through large, moss-covered boulders towards the eastern edge of the large spire. "Bats eat insects, not fodder." She whispered. "Wasn't biology required where you did your undergraduate work?"

"It's just an expression. After last night aren't you thankful just to be alive?"

Jennifer moved forward until she stood beside Lee. She reached for his arm. "I'm not really a complainer, Lee. And...I am thankful that...that you kept me alive."

He met her gaze. After what she had been through, she was hardly a complainer. Were those tears in her eyes?

He slid his arm through hers until their hands touched and clasped. "Jenn, thank you for keeping me alive, too. But in a few moments, you might not be so thankful I brought you up here. I'm taking you to the best hiding place I know, but getting there...well, it's a bit dicey."

She squeezed his hand. "It's better if you don't scare me in advance. Just lead me there and let me get frightened on my own. It minimizes the fright time."

He wanted to prepare her for what was coming— to encourage her. Instead, he followed her advice.

Fifty yards beyond the large cave they crawled over the eastern shoulder of the large spire.

Jennifer made the steep climb without problems.

At the top, he guided her around a large rock.

She gasped when she realized where they stood. The seventy-foot precipice at Jennifer's feet formed the partially hidden, southeast face of the spire.

She looked down to the bottom then returned her wide-eyed gaze to his. "Dicey?"

"A little. But don't worry. We've rolled sevens all night long."

She didn't laugh. His comment drew only a glaring frown.

Evidently she didn't appreciate a good pun.

He gave her his most convincing smile. "We've got ten minutes to climb down to the ledge."

"It's at least seventy-five feet to the bottom. I can't—"

"Yes you can, Jenn. You showed me the incredible things you're capable of several times last night. It's only thirty feet down to the ledge."

"Just stop. If you keep buttering me up I'll be too slippery to hang on to anything."

Maybe he was wrong about puns.

The thirty-foot descent bordered on real rock climbing. Not the rope and piton variety, but still serious enough to get a person killed if they made a mistake.

He prayed she would show the same spirit he had seen so far. The spirit that won his—there would be time to think about that later.

At least, he hoped so.

He crouched at the edge of the rock face below them. His gaze moved from handhold to handhold, foothold to foothold, tracing the path he'd used as a child. Satisfied, he slid his body over the edge.

Jennifer gasped again.

When his feet hit the small ledge four feet below he looked into wide eyes and a frown. He smiled and whirled his hand in a circle. "Turn around. Lie on your stomach and slide your feet over the edge. I'll guide them onto the ledge beside me."

After two aborted starts, she made it onto the ledge.

Lee kept an arm snug around her waist.

She was trembling. Jennifer stared down the rock towards its base. The bottom was seventy feet below them. "I only have two phobias, fear of heights and of raging water."

"There's no raging water around here and it would probably help if you'd stop looking down to the bottom. Just look where we're climbing. Watch my hands and feet closely. If I place my right foot or hand on a hold you do the same. The same goes for the left hand and foot. If you get crossed up you could get stuck." He didn't say the rest of it, but she got it.

"Or fall. I get it," she whispered back. "OK, you lead. And Lee?"

"Yes?"

"Please don't take any big steps or I will get stuck."

He whispered softly into her ear. "I'll make you a regular freeway down this rock wall, Jenn."

Her body became rigid. "After last night I don't think I ever want to see another freeway."

He removed his arm and climbed down four steps. "OK, no freeways, no semis, no SUVs—just a quiet little lane."

Jennifer's eyes widened until they created horizontal lines on her forehead. Her body leaned inward towards the rock. Each movement was slow, tentative.

He prayed she would continue following him. If she froze they could become sitting ducks on the side of this rock.

For their descent, he chose to climb down a V-shaped notch in the rock. The indentation permitted him to overlap his body with Jennifer's for most of the climb. Without climbing gear the notch provided the safest path of descent. Being inside the notch might also reduce her fear.

Ten feet down the rock he paused, waiting for Jennifer to descend so their bodies overlapped. When he looked up to monitor her progress he noticed the smooth soles of her shoes. That concerned him.

Jennifer stopped.

That concerned him, too. He watched until he saw her testing handholds.

At least she hadn't frozen.

While he waited for her he strengthened his grip on the rock face. He looked down and repositioned his feet.

A scraping noise near his head startled him.

Jennifer gasped. Or was it a stifled scream?

Lee glanced up.

Her right foot had slipped from its foothold.

His whole body became rigid.

The weight of Jennifer's right side jerked hard on her right hand. It ripped loose from its hold. Her right side was completely detached from the rock. She swung away from it like a door, hinged on her left hand and foot. Her body hung over...nothing.

The strain on Jennifer's left hand tore it loose from its hold. She gasped loudly, but suppressed the scream a weaker person could not have stifled

His right hand shot upward. For one brief moment her front side came within reach. He squeezed his left hand hold with all his strength. With his right he clawed desperately for some part of her clothing. His fingers curled around her belt.

Jennifer's body came loose from the rock. Beyond the tipping point she began to fall.

Lee pulled her body downward and in towards the rock face. Adrenaline-enhanced arm muscles jerked her body a few degrees off from the vertical force of gravity. He heard a thump and then a groan.

Her back had smashed into the rock slightly above his face. She slid down the heavy moss coating the limestone until he wedged her body between him and the rock wall. With his heart hammering he pinned her to the rock to prevent her from sliding farther.

He had brought her up to the mountaintop after promising to protect her. But, for the second time, he almost lost her. His promise, combined with the terror of what might have happened, tore at him with ferocity he had never before experienced. His feelings for this woman who would protect him, though terrified and facing her own death, suddenly grew very deep. Or perhaps he suddenly grew aware of how very deep those feelings had already grown.

Jennifer struggled to breathe. Her efforts sounded like an asthma attack.

He recognized the signs. For several years he'd heard them almost every night at football practice. He'd knocked the breath out of her when he smashed her back into the rock.

Jennifer's wizened voice rasped rough edges onto her words. "Lee, you're crushing me...my feet...are on the rock, now."

"Are you absolutely sure, Jenn?"

"Yes...and if you'll let me turn around...I'll have two good handholds."

Slowly he decreased the pressure on her body until she stood on her own with her back against the rock. He slipped one arm around her waist and allowed her to rotate her body until she faced the rock. He scrutinized every movement of her hands until she gained handholds.

When Jennifer stood secure inside the notch he took a deep breath and exhaled his panic. As he waited for the heart pounding to subside he felt Jennifer's body shaking.

He pulled her close, buried his face in her hair and held her. "You're safe now, Jenn. I won't let you fall off this rock."

She turned her head towards him. "Lee, I..." Jennifer's voice trailed off, but her eyes revealed her thoughts. They stared at something a million miles away. Though she didn't fall he realized she had experienced the horror of one of her worst phobias.

"Did I hurt you?" he whispered when she regained her composure.

"No more than you needed to. I'm OK." She leaned her head onto his shoulder and let it rest there.

He sensed they were being bonded together, not only by forces forged in the fire of shared danger, but also by something else—something that went even deeper.

Lee leaned into the rock and turned. He wanted to see her face while remaining a protective cage around her.

With a penetrating gaze she peered deeply into his

eyes.

For the second time his heart and mind were completely exposed to hers.

"Thank you, Lee…I really thought…" Her voice was heavy with emotion. She placed her cheek against his, took a deep breath, and smiled when she looked up at him. "I'm OK, now."

Seeing the bright, self-confident, young woman so vulnerable and so totally dependent upon him, placed an even heavier burden on his shoulders. Regardless, the two were still exposed on a rock face. They needed to descend to the ledge before being spotted.

"Thanks again," Jennifer whispered.

He sought an appropriate reply but could only think about the penetrating gaze from her large, brown eyes and the softness of her cheek touching his. He continued climbing down the rock watching Jennifer closely and feeling he had missed an opportunity. An opportunity to what? Answering that question would have to wait until they were safely hidden deep inside this huge monolith.

From the rock face the tiny ledge remained invisible until a person climbed down within a few feet of it. When the two reached the ledge Lee pointed to his right, towards a crevice in the rock, barely visible from where they stood. The crevice hid a narrow cave opening—one Lee and his childhood buddy discovered nearly twenty years earlier.

"Is that where we're going?" Jennifer spoke softly, nodding towards the slit in the rock.

"Yes. And, Jenn…we need to keep our voices down to a whisper from now on. These limestone formations have amazing acoustics. Acoustics that can easily betray us. Especially inside of the caves. Do you think they can find that cave?" He looked towards the hidden opening.

"I would almost bet my life they can't."

He smiled. "You don't have to. Once we're inside, you'll see we're betting our lives on a sequence of three or four events, all just as unlikely."

"I won't even bother doing the math. The odds seem pretty good to me." A genuine smile on Jennifer's face so enhanced her natural beauty he could hardly think, hardly —

I've got to get focused, or I'll get us killed.

He turned towards the cave opening. "Slide through and tell me what you see. Try to step on the rocks while we're in the cave. We don't want any footprints left in the dirt if we can avoid it."

Jennifer slid into the cave. "This is a big cavern," she said in a loud whisper.

He squeezed into the cave behind her. The opening seemed smaller than nineteen years ago when he first entered at eleven years of age. Had the petroglyphs been left undisturbed by other junior spelunkers? Enough of the good old memories. He needed to concentrate on keeping them alive.

Part of staying alive meant staying warm. He needed to convey that bit of information to Jennifer. He vacillated on his approach to what might be a sensitive subject. "We're going to be in this cave for...well, who knows how long. We won't be nearly as active in here. We both have only light jackets and the temperature will be less than fifty degrees inside. That's well within the window of — "

"Where is this discussion going, Lee?"

"We need to be alert for early signs of hypothermia. After a while, it might become as great a danger as the people shooting at us. If you feel cold, mentally sluggish, or if you start shivering, let me know."

"And what do you plan to do about it if we start getting too cold? Jumping jacks?"

In the dim light, he couldn't read her expression. "We'll have to snug—uh...get close together to stay warm."

"Brandt, are you trying to take advantage of me?"

Serious or facetious? It was too dark to see her well. He couldn't distinguish the tone of Jennifer's whisper. Whispers were like that—they didn't employ the vocal chords.

Wanting to avoid a fiery outburst he sought a safe reply. "I'm more concerned about just keeping you alive. Anything else will have to wait until we get out of here." After uttering the words he realized his implication.

He waited for a verbal assault from Jennifer. It didn't come, at least, not as a direct frontal attack.

Her face tilted up. "Have I given you any reason to believe there might be 'anything else'?"

"I...no." He wished he could have answered otherwise.

"Well," Jennifer whispered. She backed up against him and pulled his arms snugly around her. She relaxed there for several seconds. "I can handle that if we need to." She slipped away from him and continued as if nothing had transpired. "Now...where were we, Lee?"

Something had transpired. He knew it.

She did, too. Even in the semi-darkness of the cave she was obviously avoiding his gaze.

'Anything else' had become a distinct possibility.

That raised a lot of questions. For now, the questions would have to wait.

He looked towards the far side of the cavern. "There used to be a place where water dripped in here. It formed a pool."

He walked across the cavern looking for a depression in the rocks. "There it is. I don't have anything against Southerners, but I really don't want to be a redneck anymore." He sat by the pool and prepared to wash the blood from his neck and arm.

Jennifer knelt beside him and pulled his left hand from the pool of water. She took a white handkerchief from her pocket and carefully washed away the blood from his neck.

She took his right arm, bent his elbow and looked at his forearm. She shook her head. "I think your arm might be better off if we leave it alone. Who knows what might be growing in that pool of water. I won't scrub your deep abrasion with it." She released his arm. "Now...how does it feel to be a Yankee again?"

"That depends."

"Depends on what, Lee?"

"On whether I'm in this cave with a Southern belle, or not."

"It's 'or not.' Just be glad this Yankee woman can drive, or you wouldn't have gotten to this cave alive."

"You're right about the driving." He stared deeper into the cave. "We should get going. It'll take a few more minutes to reach our hideout."

"Lee?" she whispered, taking his hand. "About this hideout. I know the cave opening is hidden, but is there another way out?"

"No. If there was, the other opening couldn't possibly be as well hidden. They might use it to come in."

She dropped his hand. "We have no weapons. If they come into this cave, we're—"

"I've got a pocket knife."

"Great. Why didn't you tell me earlier? We could have used it on the freeway last night." The sarcasm in her intense, raspy whisper felt like sandpaper when only a moment ago she was so...

"Sorry. I shouldn't have—just follow me, Jenn."

"I guess I have to, don't I?"

Instead of replying he motioned ahead. "See the three branches off from this cavern?"

"Yes, two look rather promising, but the third—I would guess it goes nowhere."

"Then you'd guess wrong. And I'm counting on the people chasing us doing the same thing if they get this far."

"See," Jennifer whispered. "There's a dead end right there." She pointed to the apparent end of the small tunnel.

He walked to the end, slid to his left and disappeared into a fissure camouflaged by the irregular edge of the side wall.

A loud whisper reached his ears. "That's not funny, Lee. Where are you?"

He stepped out from the crack in the rock and extended a hand to Jennifer.

She took it.

He pulled her through the hidden crack.

They stood in a round cavern nearly fifteen feet in diameter.

He gestured towards the dark spots at the back of the cavern. "Do you see the two small dead-end tunnels?"

"Not yet. My eyes are still adjusting...OK, I see them now. I suppose one of the tunnels doesn't have a dead end."

"Neither does. But we're taking the one on the left, because it has a hidden opening a few feet inside. You can squeeze through the opening...barely. "

"Barely big enough for me? You're not going to hide me in there by myself, Lee. That's not going to happen. I'm going with you wherever—"

"Hold it. Hold it. And keep your voice down. These caves can really carry sound." He paused. "I learned to squeeze through that opening a long time ago. You put your arms through first. Pretend you're diving in. Then, when your hips feel stuck you wiggle them. You'll pop right through. I'm pretty certain the gunmen won't even try to get through unless they're certain we're inside. If one of them tries and doesn't use the right technique they'll need a man-size corkscrew to pop him out."

Jennifer dove in and crawled through until her hips stopped her. "Are you sure I won't get stuck?"

"Pretend you're doing the hula."

"I don't dance, Lee."

"Not even to save your life?"

She didn't answer.

After a few gyrations of her lower body, Jennifer slipped through and sat on the floor of the tunnel. "Amazing."

Lee stuck his head in. "I've always thought that about the hula, too."

It was too dark to see the expression on her face, but it didn't look like a smile.

He scanned the ceiling of the tunnel. "Most places this deep inside the rock are totally dark. But here there are a lot of cracks in the rock above us. During the daytime you can usually find enough light to get around. Let your eyes adjust for a couple of minutes before you start moving. But be careful, because you can't see the floor of the cave very well. It's easy to trip and take a tumble. I've done it."

"I can already see a little."

He assumed the diving position then pushed his arms and head through the hole in the rock. His shoulders had broadened over the past ten years. "I'm stuck. See if you can pull my left hand hard enough for my shoulders to twist and slide through."

Jennifer pulled.

His shoulders didn't budge. "Try again. Pull harder this time."

Jennifer set her feet for maximum leverage and pulled.

His shoulders slipped through the tight spot. He wiggled his hips a couple of times. They followed. He fell onto the floor of the cave.

She stood staring down at him. "I can't believe you did that. I barely squeezed through, and my hips are—well..."

He stood. "Unless I left a lot of evidence when you pulled me through I don't think the goons will follow us in here. Nobody but my buddy could find us here and he lives halfway across the country."

"So you're sure we're safe?"

"What do you think?"

"I think we are, but as I said, if by chance they happen to come in, we're dead...unless you know of an alternate way out."

"I've never found another way out of here. But don't worry. They're not going to find the way in."

"What if they see the rocks and the caves and decide to look systematically in every cave for us? Won't they eventually get here?"

"Considering there are six or seven limestone outcroppings on this mountain, having a total of fifteen caves I know about, and considering how hidden this cavern is, I would bet my life they can't find us."

"You're right, Lee. I'm a little paranoid after last night when they kept finding us on the roads. The police surely know we're missing after the bombing and the gunshots. I don't think they have enough time to find us before the police or the FBI find them."

Lee rubbed his chin for a few seconds. "Yeah. But like you said, we're betting our lives, so we need a plan—some kind of last-ditch effort to save ourselves—something we do if we hear them in this cave. Got any ideas?"

Jennifer flashed him a glance. It turned into a stare. "I thought you would suggest praying."

Why did she—it doesn't matter why.

God had opened the door again

"We should be doing that now. Prayer is for all circumstances all of the time not just for dire emergencies."

Jennifer stepped close hardly two feet away. "If you really believe that shouldn't you pray right now?"

Her nearness disrupted his thoughts. "I...yes. That would be appropriate."

Jennifer looked up into his face, and then down at her feet. "Lee, can I...would you ..." There was a long pause.

Where did the shy woman come from?

"What, Jenn?"

"I...want to hear you pray...if you don't mind."

"So you don't want another screaming, silent one?" He didn't wait for a reply. "Neither do I."

He took both of her hands. They knelt facing each other in the near darkness of the cavern. He tilted his head down. Their foreheads touched. He tensed, but relaxed when Jennifer left her head resting lightly against his.

With Jennifer this close how could he concentrate? But sensing this might be an important moment for her, he prayed—first silently.

Lord, please let this be a good one. "Father, we thank You for being a God who wants to hear us talk to You and One who answers when we do. I thank You so much for keeping us safe through the night. Thanks for bringing Jennifer to help me. Her work will probably save many innocent lives. And Randy—I pray You will keep him safe. We know these people shot at him and we don't know what happened. But we commit him to Your care, Father. Please lead the police and FBI to find the gunmen and their cohorts who are plotting evil. Protect us while we hide in this cave. When it's the right time show us the way out, so we can complete the work Jenn started—the work to thwart the terrorist plot and bring all involved to justice. Finally, Father, make Yourself known to Jenn, so she can have the relationship You have intended all along."

As he closed the prayer, he felt wet drops splash on his hand.

Jennifer removed her hands and in the shadowy darkness appeared to be wiping her eyes. She remained kneeling for a few moments. "Thanks, Lee. I...I didn't know it was...like that."

Shy, nervous—uncharacteristic of the confident, young woman he observed closely for the past several hours.

"Like what?"

"Like...talking to my father. He died two years ago."

"I'm so sorry, Jenn. About praying, well...that's how it is for me. But there's one—"

"No buts, Lee. I told you I don't like buts."

The fiery-spirited Jennifer had returned. Which was the real Jennifer? Maybe both?

9

Abdul pored over the limestone monolith crowning the mountain. He saw caves everywhere. "He thinks he is clever."

Ratib scanned the numerous caves and shook his head. "He *is* clever, Abdul. They have no weapons so their only chance was to hide. We see many caves, but there may still be others we cannot see."

"Be that as it may, we must find Brandt and the woman quickly and we cannot look in all of these caves. Maram, go back to the vehicle. Bring our flashlight, our sound gun, and the Voice Activity Detector. Make sure that you get all the cables so we can connect the VAD and the sound gun."

"VAD," Maram mocked Abdul, imitating his voice. "You make it sound so sophisticated. It is just an old telephone you dismantled."

"It is a very new telephone. From it I created the VAD."

"Whatever." Maram made no effort to comply with his order. "Ratib knows what you want and he can run faster than me. Send him."

"Do as I say. Ratib and I will guard the caves at the base of the rock until you return. When we couple the sound gun with the VAD you will see who is clever." Abdul's patience with Maram was gone and his need for her…it was waning.

Maram resented making the steep climb.

He could hear her grumbling as she set out.

"I solidified the alliance with the cartel. I went in first. Winning their confidence required haraam—forbidden things—still, they treat me like an infidel, because I am a woman." Lately, Maram was always grumbling.

Abdul watched her walk carelessly down the steep slope. When she stumbled and fell, scraping her arms, she spewed a long stream of complaints interspersed with Spanish profanity. The influence of the drug lords. Still, she did his bidding. But for how much longer would she do so? Could he trust her any longer? He rephrased the question, making it a statement. *I will trust her no longer.*

When Maram was out of earshot he turned to Ratib. "I want you to keep this in mind. If we think the two might possibly escape we must shoot to kill. But if possible, I want to trap and capture them. We need to find out how much they know and who, if anyone, they talked to before they left the building."

"Suppose we capture them and they refuse to talk?"

"If we catch them we can make them talk. We will simply start torturing the woman. Brandt will talk."

"How do you know that? Isn't he a Christian? Sometimes they—"

"Do you know nothing? These Christians value women more than men. If we torture the woman Brandt will tell us whatever we want to know. But I did not want to discuss this with Maram present. I think she spent too many months with the drug lords. Her thinking has been corrupted and she might not approve of our tactics. She no longer thinks like a true Muslim woman."

"I believe you are right, Abdul. Might this be her last mission?"

"Her very last. Maram's mission will end when we return to the SUV. After we kill Brandt and the woman we will have no further need for Maram. However, if she objects to torturing the woman as I suspect she might, we will kill her immediately."

"I agree. We have no choice. But tell me, Abdul, how do you plan to find the two infidels using the listening devices?"

"I will take the output of the sound gun and attach it to the input of the VAD. We must work quickly though, because the sound gun only runs for about four hours on fully charged batteries and we do not know how much charge is left in them."

Ratib frowned as he stared at the limestone spire. "I know we must hurry. But what is our strategy for finding this man, Lee Brandt, and the woman?"

"Speaking in caves is like talking through a hose. If we listen at the mouth of the cave we will hear them from the end of a hose."

"But what if they are very quiet?"

"That is why we attach the VAD to the amplified sound from the gun. Any sound from human vocal chords can be detected separately from background noise. All VoIP phones have basic voice-detection capability. For whisper detection I borrowed a chip from one of our friends who works for an Asian cellphone manufacturer."

Abdul was proud of his ingenious invention. Using an off-the-shelf phone he employed his software skills to tweak the firmware, splicing in the whisper detection. The final part, amplifying the input signal using a sound gun, only required bypassing the phone's microphone permitting the sound gun to provide the input. A telephone technician showed him how to configure the bypass,and even told him what electronic components he needed including the addition of the LED voice-indicator light to complete it.

Abdul originally designed the device for eavesdropping and use in the border-crossing tunnels. Later, he found other applications. This day's application didn't require hearing what Lee and the woman said. He only needed to detect their voices to locate them. He expected the VAD to perform very well in these caves. In fact, today's use of the VAD might be his crowning—

"Abdul, are you listening?"

He must stop basking in his glories. "Yes, Ratib. Please continue."

"So...we point the sound gun into the mouth of each cave for a while and continue until we locate their hiding place?"

"That is correct. Now, while we wait for Maram to return we will remain quiet and listen for any sounds indicating where to start searching."

For nearly forty-five minutes Abdul waited quietly, but impatiently, for Maram's return. His mood grew fouler by the minute. Precious time trickled away. He knew the search undoubtedly under way for Brandt and the woman would soon bring the police somewhere near this mountain. The two must be dead or removed from here before the police found their vehicles. With Brandt and the woman out of the picture, provided the two hadn't disclosed details of his plan, their mission would still succeed.

Ratib shifted, and then broke their self-imposed silence. "Abdul, what do you suppose the woman's role was? The news we heard on the car radio gave no details about Jennifer Akihara."

"I know about Lee Brandt's skills. I worked with him for several weeks. He could not have located our computer specialists and pinged their machines from his work location. He needed the woman to accomplish that. The radio news report said she has a degree in computing security. So we must assume she has the necessary skills to trace even well-disguised Internet communications."

"If so, what she did was very impressive. Could she be of any value to us or our associates?"

"Ratib, she is an infidel and she knows too much. Her only value to us lies in her death. Even if she has great skills we could never trust her. She could deceive us too easily. And, as I already said, she is an infidel. She must die."

A clattering sound announced Maram's return. She collapsed at Abdul's feet breathing hard, but she held the sound equipment and the flashlight. "Here...are your...play toys, Abdul." She spoke between heavy breaths and made no attempt to disguise her disdain.

Abdul glared at her. "Then let us play," he quipped, but his icy stare conveyed no humor. "When I use the equipment both of you must remain absolutely silent. If I detect any human voice activity I want it to be theirs. Do you understand?"

Ratib nodded.

Maram stared at Abdul for several seconds, and then nodded.

With a sigh, Abdul subdued his anger at Maram before it could turn to rage. "We will move from cave to cave spending no more than five minutes at any opening. You must help me keep track of where we have been. Also we must look for other caves."

Abdul started by monitoring the largest cave at the base of the limestone spire. An hour later they listened at the mouth of the last visible cave. But they found no traces of human voices.

"Abdul, is the device working properly?" Ratib asked.

"Yes, I know it is working."

Ratib stared at the cobbled voice-detection equipment with his hands on his hips. "Can it detect them even when hidden deep inside these massive rocks?"

"I have no doubt that it can. They must know of a cave we have not yet found. Maram, hold the sound gun while Ratib and I explore the sides of the rock."

Ratib headed for the southwest corner of the large spire.

Maram walked with him for a few yards towards the northeast corner of the huge rock.

He glanced at her as she sat down on a flat slab of limestone. She set her weapon down and slumped forward dropping the sound equipment into her lap.

Abdul's gaze explored every part of the easternmost shoulder of the huge monolith. While he looked high up on the rock towards the pinnacle of the spire he saw something in the periphery of his vision. He turned his head in response. The bright red LED on the VAD blinked out a most welcome message.

"Maram, be very still."

Maram froze in her sitting position on the rock. When she stiffened the sound gun slid from her lap. She grabbed it just before it toppled to the rocks below.

"You fool!" He exclaimed. He took a deep breath

and sought a kinder tone of voice. "Maram, please place the sound gun in your lap exactly as it was before it fell."

Maram carefully positioned the gun pointing it to the shoulder of the rock nearly fifty feet above her.

He sighted along the sound gun until he focused on a slight depression in the rock near the top of the cliff face where the morning sun now lit the upper portion of the spire. He scanned the lower portion of the cliff. They could not climb to the suspicious location without rock-climbing gear.

Above the depression a little to his left, Abdul noticed a discolored area on the limestone. He walked to the base of the rock and looked closely at it. Moss was scraped off the rock above the depression. At his feet Abdul saw bits of green moss scattered among the shards of limestone. Someone climbed down from the top of the rock to the depression. The depression must be a ledge. What did it host? Perhaps the opening to a cave? "Let me have the sound gun, Maram. Be absolutely silent."

Abdul pointed the sensor directly at the depression on the rock and waited. In less than minute the light on the VAD again blinked out the portentous message.

"Maram, keep monitoring that spot on the rock above us. Do you see it?"

"Yes, I am tired, but I am not blind."

"I am going to get Ratib. I think we have found our mice. Now it is time to behave as all cats do."

10

Lee sat facing Jennifer in the small cavern. In the darkness, her face became only a vague, shadowy form, eliminating a distraction he could not afford. He needed to focus on their escape plan.

"If somehow they stumble across this cave and start getting too close for comfort—"

"They're already too close for comfort." Jennifer's whisper raised a semitone or two.

"Yeah. You're right about that. But wouldn't you like to know who they really are? Ram had to be a terrorist, but beyond that we—"

"That might satisfy your curiosity, but it wouldn't improve our situation now, would it?"

"At least we would die knowing who killed us," he replied without thinking.

Jennifer recoiled from him. "I thought you said God must have more planned for me to do." She wanted some kind of assurance.

Was God opening another door?

"I think He does have more planned for you and me. He brought us this far so I can't believe He will let the goons kill us." He paused, and then stepped through the open door. "But, you don't have to live in fear of death. There is Someone you can know Who has overcome death. He can overcome it for you, too."

Jennifer slid forward. "I would really like to believe that. However, I'm not to that point yet." She stared at the cavern wall. "I suppose, though, if someone wholeheartedly believed it, it would make them absolutely fearless, wouldn't it?" Her voice sounded different, like a small child, but the darkness hid much of her body language.

He focused on her question. "That's right in theory. For me though, it just makes me fear less, not fearless. I don't fear my death because I know Who lies just beyond that door. The thing that still scares me is what might happen leading to my death. And with these goo—"

"Can we talk about something other than death right now? I would rather live to see these guys arrested for attempted murder or, better yet, tried in a military court." Jennifer had changed the subject again.

And he had blown it.

Sorry, Lord. But this woman you sent my way is... Sorry again. That excuse didn't fly the first time You heard it.

"In order to make sure we live to see them brought to justice we'd better come up with an emergency plan, a plan we invoke if we hear them in this cave. Got any ideas?"

"As a matter of fact I do." Her gaze returned to his face. "But first there's something I want to ask you."

"OK...uh...what's that?"

"Don't worry. I think you can handle this one." She paused for several seconds. "When did you start calling me Jenn instead of Jennifer?"

A video clip stored in his memory played. "Things were happening pretty fast while you were driving. I guess Jennifer took too long to say. Jenn seemed to work better at the time. Do you want me to call you Jennifer?"

"No, it's OK. I've just never allowed anyone to shorten my name except…" Pause. "Dad."

"So you're saying it's OK for me to be something like a father figure?" *Please tell me I didn't say that.* Jennifer was recalling the painful loss of her father and he was thinking about—he wasn't thinking, just being stupid.

"That's not what I mean…I wouldn't want you to be my father because I…" There was another pause. "Because, well, Dad is dead, and I said I don't want to talk about death right now. So, about the backup plan, which I'm sure we won't need, have you ever slid under that big overhanging rock?" She pointed to the dark slit near the floor in the rear left quadrant of the cavern.

What was she about to say before changing the subject?

He couldn't let his mind run wild with possibilities. He'd better concentrate on the subject at hand. "Under that overhang? No. My buddy and I never went under that rock. I do know there's less than a foot of clearance under the front edge, because I stuck my head in once. I only saw darkness and didn't have a light at the time, or the inclination to explore it."

He decided against explaining his disinclination to explore the slit under the rock. Telling her how he'd freaked out in one of these caves—a full-blown, claustrophobic, panic attack, could serve no good purpose. He had bailed out into total darkness that day. Fifteen feet up on a chimney wall inside a big cavern. But truthfully, he didn't even know how high up he was. He'd just bailed.

He couldn't afford to panic today. He brought Jennifer into this cave, told her she would be safe, and he must deliver on that promise. If he failed to keep the promise his only consolation would be he wouldn't live to regret it.

Lee looked at the dark slit barely visible under the overhanging rock. To him, it had claustrophobia written on it in neon lights. Nevertheless, the small cavern offered nothing else to check—nothing hinting of a way to hide, or escape.

He prayed softly. "Please, don't let me get stuck in there, God, and please...no panic attacks."

Jennifer's voice came from behind him. "What did you say?"

"Uh...I'm going to check out your hiding place...you know, the crack under the big rock." Was he practicing deception with Jennifer? He shoved the thought from his mind.

"Be careful, Lee. I'm going to sit here and listen for...hopefully nothing."

Lee was eleven when he discovered this cavern. At the time, he doubted he could slide under the overhanging rock. At age thirty the attempt to slide under the rock required lying on his stomach and rotating his head sideways and placing his cheek on the floor of the cave.

Using his toes and hands, and the uncomfortable body position, he managed to scoot into the slit. Progress came with great difficulty. After a couple of hard bumps on the head he realized the underside of the rock was not smooth. It was too dark to see anything, so he started feeling the rock above with the backs of his hands.

After nearly five minutes of scooting and periodically getting stuck he still hadn't found an end to the crack. He lay spread-eagled about fifteen feet in engaged in a fierce firefight with claustrophobia. That "can't breathe" thought threatened to explode like a bomb in his mind, sending him into insane behavior, or perhaps into insanity itself.

On the verge of panic, only Jennifer's dependence on him kept him from running up the white flag. If he lost it completely and started screaming like a mad man he would probably lose Jennifer, too.

Barely man-sized, this crack was worse than the MRI tube the doctor placed him in after a hard collision with a wall knocked him out on a racquetball court. The cave was much quieter, but he would prefer the MRI tube any day. In fact he would prefer—his heart raced and he began rapid, shallow panting.

Lord, please help me. I have to get out of here now.

His first scream was still embryonic, growing fast in the womb of his conscious mind, when Jennifer's voice reached him.

"How's it going in there?" Her whisper echoed all around him. Her voice had wonderful tranquilizing qualities.

The scream died somewhere short of his vocal chords. He took a deep breath and tried to relax. When he reached up to feel the rock his hand felt nothing. Then the back of his forearm struck a sharp edge, the end of the overhanging rock.

Thank you, Lord.

"Jenn, I think there's an opening back here. I'm going to slide into it and let my eyes adjust. In a few minutes I'll know what's back here."

"OK, but please try to hurry. The scooting noise you're making echoes all around in the cavern. I can't tell which direction it's coming from. It makes me really nervous."

Not as nervous as my screaming would have made you.

He took a deep breath and exhaled. "It's OK, Jenn. The scooting part is over for now. Check back with me in about five minutes. I might have some good news."

"OK, five minutes. But...please hurry."

****

Jennifer sat alone in the darkness of their hideout waiting for Lee to explore the opening he found. Though danger threatened Lee dominated her thoughts. There was an obvious, strong attraction between them. But Jennifer's feelings went deeper than mere attraction—so deep they frightened her.

She couldn't stop the smile that spread across her face when she recalled how Lee first reacted when they met in Howie's office. He acted like every other guy, like an idiot. But he hadn't treated her like any other guy. He encouraged her, protected her—did that signify something deeper?

He possessed a strong faith.

She thought faith in God was a false crutch.

But Lee's faith strengthened him and his strength carried her through several moments of crisis.

Jennifer jumped at a sound coming from somewhere she couldn't locate. She listened for a few moments, but heard no voices—nothing.

It must be Lee exploring the cavern.

Guys had always brought her trouble. That started when she turned thirteen. Because of one guy who brought trouble she usually carried a gun. But the trouble that came with Lee wasn't his doing.

She listened for a few moments. No more noises.

In a minute or two she would check with Lee to

see what he found. But what she found in him mystified her. It drew her. It seemed to her Lee's life was built around relationships, even one with God. She merely communicated with a few people, but Lee lived in community with many people. They respected him—even Howie—Howie who set her up—Howie who tried to fill in for her dad. Did Howie somehow know she needed Lee?

If she believed in God like Lee believed she would ask Him to show her what was happening here. But that was a silly contemplation. They might never get out of these caves alive. That's what she should be asking God about—what a person needs to know before they die.

Would He really answer if she asked?

****

Abdul led the three as they entered the occupied tunnel. He stopped suddenly and stared at the confusing rock structure in front of him. His gaze locked on a small opening that appeared to penetrate deeper into the rock. "Maram, come here."

She stepped beside Abdul, who continued to study the hole. "Maram, you are the only one of us I am sure can pass through this opening. Slide through and I will pass you the light...but wait, Maram."

"Make up your mind, Abdul."

Maram seemed increasingly irritated with each command he gave her. It mattered little. Only a few more commands remained until he gave her the last one. "I need to examine these marks on the rocks." Abdul pointed the light through the hole. "There are also marks on the cave floor. So, they did not seek another tunnel after all. Go now, Maram."

"Always it is me who gets the dirty work." After some wiggling of her body, Maram slipped through the hole and fell onto the cave floor beyond it.

Abdul shoved the light at her. "No, Maram. The real dirty work will begin shortly and I will be the one doing it."

Dirty work for which you have made me work much too hard, Lee Brandt.

When Maram reached back for the sound equipment, Ratib pushed it towards her. The parabolic dish clanked against the sides of the hole. "The sound gun does not fit through the hole. What should we do, Abdul?"

Abdul shrugged. "It no longer matters. See...the batteries have died. But we still have the light and they cannot be far ahead. Maram, take our guns while Ratib and I squeeze through this hole. If Lee Brandt thinks this obstruction will stop us he is a fool."

Ratib struggled to work his body through the small hole Maram had easily slipped through. When Ratib fell exhausted onto the cave floor Abdul took his turn. More strongly built than Ratib, he became stuck in the small opening. Skin scraped from his arms and one shoulder when he forced his body violently through the opening.

Abdul clenched his jaw and stared at his bleeding abrasions. "Lee will pay, skin for skin. Or perhaps the girl will pay," he whispered.

****

A sound startled Jennifer from her musings.

Voices echoed through the tunnel. They came from

somewhere near the entrance to the cave, not from Lee.

They're in the cave almost here.

Her heartbeat jarred her. Her breathing became panting. News clips replayed in her mind—videos of the atrocities terrorists and drug lords inflicted on their captives. The images in her mind drove her deeper into panic. These evil men beheaded people. Dismembered them and—she had to stop this enumeration.

It wasn't supposed to happen like this. She knew they might be killed. If so, she thought she would die beside Lee. Not alone in a cave. In the dark. Without Lee. Without God? No. She needed them both.

Please, God, help me.

Jennifer shrank to the back of the cavern. She stood next to the overhanging rock. Her hands trembled when she placed them on the floor of the cave. Her arms shook, barely able to support her weight, as she lowered her body to the opening under the rock.

Footsteps reverberated through the chamber.

When she slid under the rock the darkness of the cavern exploded into light.

11

Lee's panic subsided. He sat on the edge of a cavern of unknown size waiting for his vision to adjust. Nearly five minutes passed and he began to notice strange things as he glanced around. An infinite number of shades of black existed between darkness and total darkness. Only prolonged exposure to darkness in a cave without a light could teach him that. But he wasn't completely without light, because—

It came from above. Light was shining down. It drew his gaze upward to its source. If it wasn't light, it was at least one of those lighter shades of black.

When Lee tilted his head to look upward, he detected a faint light high above. Hoping to see the sides of the chimney wall, he lowered his gaze, permitting his eyes to readjust to the darkness. As he waited a small down draft tickled the hairs on the back of his hands and neck. A puff of slightly fresher air descended upon him. Air from the land of the free. The place he must take Jennifer.

After a few seconds Lee could distinguish the lower part of the cavern walls. This cavern was large, at least fifty feet across. He moved carefully to one side and began examining the wall. He surveyed the lower portion. They could climb it easily, but the mid and upper portions were shrouded in shadows. A faint hope began growing, but two nagging questions remained. Could they make it to the top? If so, could they actually climb out?

If this represents a way out of this cave for Jennifer, please show me, God. There's no way I would try to take her up this wall unless I know it's a way of escape. The climb would terrify her, or worse. Please give me some direction.

****

Abdul followed close behind Ratib, who carried the flashlight. Moving deeper into the bowels of the limestone spire, the three continued to track their quarry. In a couple of minutes they approached a place where the tunnel widened.

This must be the place.

Abdul pulled Ratib to a stop. He brought the three of them into a huddle. "When we enter, find them with the light, Ratib. Maram, be ready with your weapon. When I signal we will enter."

On Abdul's cue the three stepped into the small cavern. Ratib swept it with the light. But what Abdul saw disturbed him. "The cave goes no further. They could not have disappeared. Give me the light, Ratib."

They could not lose these two. It would mean losing access to data for all of National Aerospace's weapon systems. Anger threatened to cloud his thinking. He took the flashlight and explored every nook until all that remained was a narrow slit near the cave floor in the rear left quadrant of the cavern. He pointed at the spot. "Be quiet and listen."

After a few seconds Ratib pointed towards the narrow opening near the floor of the cave and nodded. Ratib's hearing was sharper than his. Smiling now, Abdul knelt and bent low. After placing his face on the cave floor, Abdul shined the flashlight into the narrow opening under the rock.

****

Lee had prayed about climbing the chimney wall, but so far God hadn't—he gasped when a hand grabbed his shoulder. He whirled to defend himself. A soft hand gently touched his face. He heard rapid breathing.

"I slid through because they're in the cavern. I don't think they saw me slip out." She wrapped herself around him as if she wanted to merge with the space he occupied.

Lee could feel her arms trembling and her body convulsing as Jennifer tried simultaneously to catch her breath and stifle her sobs. He held her until the sobbing subsided.

They could afford no more time. "Well I guess we can consider the backup plan invoked," he whispered.

Jennifer still clung tightly to him.

"What backup plan?"

"Yours. I'm just thankful you convinced me to slide through Claustrophobia Cleft to find this cavern, or we would be—well, I'd hate to think where we would be. Did you say they had a light?"

"Yes, the beam almost hit me as I slid under the overhang. Lee, I think you'd better tell me the rest of my backup plan. All I remember was slide under that big overhanging rock. That's not going to cut it here."

Good. Some of Jennifer's spunk is returning.

She would soon need all of it.

"Come on, let's go." He pulled her towards the cavern wall.

"Go where?" She whispered, resisting his tug.

"You may not believe this, but I asked to be shown a safe way out of this cave, and then you grabbed my shoulder. I wanted to be convinced this was the way to go, or I wasn't going to take you there. Well, I'm convinced."

Lee stopped and faced Jennifer.

She clamped her hands onto his arms. "Take me there? 'There' is beginning to sound ominous. Where is 'there'?"

He put his hand under her chin and gently lifted. "What do you see?"

"Oh, Lee, there's light up there...but I can barely see it." She sounded excited, but her grip on his arm tightened until it threatened to cut off his circulation.

He could feel her trembling again before he withdrew his hand.

A climb to who knows what, in near total darkness, was going to tax her to her limits. But her limits had surprised him several times. Perhaps they would again.

"As far as I was able to see, Jenn, the chimney wall looked very climbable."

She became completely still. "How far was that?"

This wasn't a time to get into specific heights. "About one-fourth of the way up."

"One-fourth of what? You've seen I don't do well with heights—acrophobia."

"OK. I won't tell you how high and you won't be able to see anything below, only the light ahead of us where—"

"That's not funny, Lee." She whispered more loudly than was prudent.

"Sorry, but—"

"I don't like buts, Lee."

"But, Jenn, this is where we finally get out of the cave and get help. We've already lost the better part of a minute. C'mon. I'll climb with you each step of the way. We've been shown the way out, but we've got to choose to take it."

Jennifer kept a firm grip on Lee's left hand while he led her to the base of the chimney wall. Before they started their ascent he needed to warn her about what waited a short way up the wall—something ladies might not tolerate well. "Jennifer, you—"

"What happened to Jenn?"

"This is more of a Jennifer message."

"You said this was a way out. It's beginning to sound more like a 'but', introducing something unpleasant."

"You could say that. Just be extra careful after we're up"—he stopped himself before adding the words, twenty-five feet—"after we've climbed for a couple minutes."

"Be extra careful? How?"

"Just be careful because that's where the slime from algae, fungi, and bacteria starts. It will get a bit slippery. That offensive odor you smell...it will get a lot worse."

"Just start, Lee. I don't want to hear any more about the chimney except what's at the top—light, freedom, and safe—"

Jennifer gasped as a beam of light shattered the darkness.

It glared from the slit under the rock leading to their cavern. With it came muffled voices. Excited voices.

Lee grabbed her arm, stepped up onto a ledge three feet above the cave floor and yanked Jennifer up beside him. Less than a second later the light beam sliced through the spot where their feet had been.

He leaned into her ear. "We've got to move quickly," he whispered. "Faster. Go. I'm right behind you."

They scrambled up the rock wall at breakneck speed.

Twenty feet up the wall Jennifer paused for a few seconds. She was breathing hard.

"Jenn, they may try to enter this cavern. We have to get to the top before they can get in."

He didn't have the heart to tell her they had a least fifty more feet of vertical climbing to reach the top. It didn't appear likely that they would make it before—

"Stuck."

They heard the word distinctly, though it came wrapped in a thick accent Lee couldn't identify. He might have laughed under other circumstances, but right now "stuck" was the only thing between them and being blown off the chimney wall by automatic weapons.

"Jenn, keep moving as fast as you can, they're—"

"I know, stuck."

They reached the worst of the algae and the smell ripened. The cave had a bad case of halitosis. The wall became slippery and the goop stuck onto Lee's hands.

Jennifer's foot slipped. She started sliding down the wall.

Lee reached for her, but she caught herself on her previous foothold. His heart pounded.

Jennifer began panting. Was she hyperventilating?

They had to change their climbing strategy or they'd never make it to the top.

"Let me guide your hands and feet now. Ignore

the odor."

He moved up, surrounded Jennifer, and placed his hands over hers. They climbed moving their hands synchronously to new holds. After reaching them Lee wiped away the slime before it could lubricate Jennifer's fingers. He found new footholds and guided her feet onto them. This kept Jennifer relatively safe, but they were climbing far too slowly to reach the top before the goons entered the cavern. They needed "stuck" to last a while longer.

Below them came furious grunts and wild motions of the light beam as the gunman tried to get unstuck from the jaws of the giant rock vise that nearly clamped on him. Loud cries came from below.

They still needed to climb twenty or thirty feet to reach the top, but the sunlight seeping into the chimney gave them better visibility. There was less slime. But his mind raced searching for a solution to what looked more and more like an intractable problem. How to avoid becoming targets on a wall.

Jennifer turned. "If they get through we're sitting ducks on this wall."

She just had to say that.

He didn't reply.

A bright yellow oval flashed onto the cave wall opposite them.

Jennifer gasped.

"Stuck" was over. Though the light shone on the opposite chimney wall it might expose them at any moment.

Lee glanced up at the cavern wall then placed his mouth close to Jennifer's head. "Quick. Move up to your left...about ten feet."

She immediately made the adjustment. Climbing

with more confidence now she scrambled upward to where the light from above created a shadow. Some irregularity in the wall.

As they approached it he prayed it was enough to stop light, bullets, or both.

The yellow oval systematically explored the chimney walls from bottom to top. After each pass up the wall it moved one position in a counterclockwise direction.

Lee hoped all the people below had their eyes fixed upon that oval. If even one stopped following the bright light and let their eyes adjust to the diffuse light illuminating the rest of the cavern they would see Jennifer and him on the wall of the cave.

Fortunately, the goons started at the north wall, opposite their position. The light's vertical sweeping progressed through northwest to the west wall. When it approached the south Jennifer broke free of his protective cage around her. She scrambled to the protrusion on the cavern wall.

He looked down. The yellow oval shone brightly on the base of the chimney directly below them. He watched it move slowly upward. He glanced up at Jennifer.

She was gone. In a second or two, Jennifer's head popped out from the cave wall. She had found a place to hide.

He climbed at a near sprint to reach her.

The light moved steadily upward. It slowed as it approached his feet.

A loud click reverberated through the cavern. Someone loaded a cartridge into the chamber of a gun.

His body tensed. He expected to hear shots. To feel bullets tear through his flesh. He tried to keep moving—anything to spoil their aim.

The shots hadn't started.

Something, or someone, delayed them.

Jennifer looked down at him. In the diffuse light the whites of her eyes shone brightly, completely encircling her pupils.

He leaped to a foothold near her.

She grabbed his left wrist. An incredibly strong arm pulled him into a slit in the cave wall.

How did she do that?

"Get in here." Jennifer's voice, though it was a whisper, sounded as if it came from a wild animal, full of fury.

She hooked his neck with one arm and grabbed a handful of his jacket with the other hand. In one violent jerk she jammed him into the crevice beside her.

His body pressed tightly against Jennifer. Something about the law of the conservation of matter flashed through his mind followed by an accusation against Jennifer for violating it. This small woman continued to amaze him with her resilience and her heart.

The flashlight's oval beam now moved beside them. It illuminated the fingers on his right hand when it passed by on its way to the top of the chimney.

Lee jerked his hand into the crevice, but the light beam jumped back to the place his hand rested a second before.

Jennifer's breathing grew louder. Then it stopped. She was holding her breath stifling the sounds of her terror.

His chest still heaved uncontrollably from the exertion and the panic.

As the light repeatedly searched the cave wall around them Lee worked his left hand into position to pull Jennifer's head onto his shoulder.

She was breathing again.

He could feel her body convulsing as she struggled to stop her sobs. He leaned his head onto hers and whispered, "It's OK, Jenn. It's all OK."

Was that really true?

It had to be.

Providentially, Jennifer had found a slab of rock nearly twelve feet high and four feet wide. It had broken loose at its base and twisted at an acute angle to the flat cave wall. The triangular slit behind it contained hardly enough space to hide one person, let alone two. Regardless, it was enough to save their lives…for the moment.

The oval light began moving up the chimney wall again in its methodical manner.

His sigh of relief was choked off when the light jumped back down the wall.

It stopped on the twisted slab of rock sheltering them. Clearly, their hiding place was under scrutiny.

Jennifer's voice came softly…pleading, "Oh please, God, no."

If that was Jennifer's first prayer, he hoped it got through. If it did, and if they somehow survived this ordeal, he suspected many more prayers would follow. That was his hope—a hope that demanded a response.

Please, God, listen to Jenn.

12

The light beam continued its systematic movement from the floor to the top of the chimney. It explored each point on the compass from south, to east, and finally back to where it began on the north side of the cavern. Next they made spot checks of areas they wanted to scrutinize further.

Lee tracked every detail of the search for them looking for any signs of —

"Have they spotted this place, yet?" At her question, his tense muscles jumped. He banged his head on the rear wall of the crevice shattering his concentration.

When he twisted his neck to look at Jennifer, he realized she was squeezed so far into the wedge-shaped crevice she could see very little of what their pursuers were doing.

He tried to shake the cobwebs from his aching head. "I don't think they could possibly see it unless they crawled up to the fifty-foot level where —"

"Fifty feet." Jennifer's whisper sounded panicky. He could feel her body trembling.

He blew it. Knowing how high on the wall they were perched she might not climb another step if they ever got the chance.

Before Lee could alleviate Jennifer's fear a voice with a heavy accent spoke from the cavern floor.

"They are not here. Let's try the other tunnel.

Perhaps some of these tunnels are connected."

"Then we must hurry. It's already 1:00 p.m. and the batteries in the light are getting weak."

After two or three minutes of sliding and grunting noises the light was gone.

They came almost directly to the cavern Lee thought could never be found. They had some way of tracking Jennifer and him. If such strong evidence led them to the hiding place the goons might still believe they were hiding in this cavern. Maybe leaving was only a pretense. One of the gunmen could be sitting in the darkness below waiting to blow them off the wall when they revealed themselves.

He needed to tell Jennifer about his suspicions before either of them did anything to compromise their hiding place. It was now so quiet in the cavern a loud whisper might be heard fifty feet below. After wiggling a bit, he put his mouth directly over Jennifer's ear. "Someone might still be down—"

"Stop it." Jennifer's hand came up from somewhere in the compressed tangle of their bodies and clamped firmly over his mouth. "You're tickling my ear. I can't stand that." Her whisper was too loud.

He waited for a moment.

No response came from below. Maybe they actually were gone.

The temptation to reply became too great. He pried Jennifer's hand from his mouth. "You mean you've never let a guy tickle your ear? You'll never get me to believe—"

Jennifer's slap closed his mouth. It also echoed throughout the cavern. Her body sagged against him, and he knew she realized what she'd done.

How could he have done that to her? If the light

came back on they'd be dead and it would be his fault. He held onto her hand and with his other arm pulled her head against his.

No whispering this time.

They both waited in silence for a response.

One minute passed. Then two minutes. No light probed their location. No sound came from below.

He placed his hand against her cheek and gently spoke. "I think they really are gone."

"And I'm very sorry for...you know," Jennifer whispered back.

"Not as sorry as you'd have been if that light had come back on."

"Don't make fun of me, Lee, I feel—"

"No. Don't apologize, Jenn. It was my fault. When I'm this close to you I get a little craz...well...you just saved my life by packing me in here like one more sardine going into a can. And you bought us a lot of time by proving the goons weren't playing a trick on us when they left. I would've kept us squished in here for another half hour and by then—"

"They might have finished searching the other caves and come back here."

He nodded and banged his head on the rocks again. "Something like that. But they have a lot of other places to search and if we can believe them their flashlight is fading fast. I don't think they'll be back here any time soon."

He led her out of the crevice to a small ledge near its opening. They could stand safely on it without clinging to the wall. Here more light seeped in from the opening above.

Jennifer leaned her back into the wall and placed her hand on his shoulder. "Why are you always trying to make me feel better about things?"

He frowned. "Sometimes I just make you feel worse. But...does making you feel better bother you?"

She removed her hand. "You didn't answer my question."

"I'm not sure I have a good answer except that, well, I just want to."

She looked up into his face. "You mean you do it because it's what you think God wants you to do?"

How much should he say? He wasn't sure. But it had to be something meaningful or it would be a lie. If, in the process, he overstepped the bounds of propriety he would deal with that later. He decided to go with the best policy, honesty. "No, Jenn, *I* want you to feel good about things."

"Oh." Jennifer lowered her head. She obviously understood both his meaning and its implications. When she raised her head her expression changed.

He wanted to read every nuance of that expression, but the dim light masked the details. He wasn't a person who swore, but at that moment, he could've cursed the darkness hiding her face from him.

On the positive side, all of the evidence he compiled so far told him Jennifer possessed a refreshing innocence. He was determined to find out if he was right and, if so, to understand how this came to be—how a woman this beautiful refrained from living a lifestyle that used her beauty to her own advantage. The solution to this puzzle might impact the entire direction of his—

"Lee, where did you go?" Jennifer peered into his face.

"Sorry, Jenn. Sometimes I get distracted."

"So I've noticed." She averted her gaze and stared

into the darkness below them.

He wanted to pursue this sudden, apparent shyness, but they'd been on this ledge far too long. "Jennifer, we need to talk about what we do when we exit this rock through the hole above us."

"And who is it you're addressing now, Jennifer or Jenn?"

A clever trap. He chose to ignore it. "I would really rather stick to one name."

"And which would that be?"

He hesitated before answering. "Jenn," he whispered.

"What?"

"Jenn."

"Oh. You mean the name?"

"Yes, I do."

She cocked her head and grinned. "I do? C'mon, Lee. Just because I let you call me Jenn doesn't mean you can start the 'I do' talk."

"But you do give me permission to call you Jenn from now on, right?"

She smiled. "Yes, I do, too."

It seemed to him that, in that moment, they passed a milestone in their relationship. Everything changed. There had been times during their panicked flight for life they'd dropped all formalities. But now all the aloofness disappeared. Despite their precarious perch and the lurking danger all felt informal, warm, and good. Still he was glad the partial darkness of the chimney hid some of his facial expressions. Light might have exposed too much.

Doesn't matter. She probably deduced it all anyway, because —

"Lee?" Jennifer waved her hand in front of his

face.

"Huh?"

"Distracted again? The plan, Lee? How are we going to get out of this cave and off of this mountain, call for help, and make sure the bad guys get caught? You know...that plan?"

Reality—the other reality—the one with danger— the one where things were not all warm and good— came flooding back.

He took a deep breath. "So, here's the plan. As long as the goons keep looking in the caves for fifteen or twenty minutes—and believe me, they still have a lot of caves to look in—this plan will work. Even if they come out in five minutes it still works."

"Do I get to have any input?"

"Of course. I value your ideas. They kept us alive last night."

She raised her eyebrows. "Last night my driving kept us alive."

"Last night, you're right about last night." He raised his index finger. "But today there is one thing that needs to happen exactly as I've planned it."

Jennifer's forehead pinched into a frown and her gaze bored into him. "I know. It's the part where you play the rear guard and stay behind to protect me like...like those Cheyenne dog soldiers?"

"I didn't know you were into history."

"I'm not. I just learned about them from a movie, Last of the—"

"Dogmen." He smiled. "So you're into adventure and romance?"

A brief smile lit her face. "I'm on this mountain with you, aren't I?"

Not only was this woman sharp, she was intuitive.

How did psychologist, Isabel Myers Briggs, classify people like her? The personality type indicator would denote a wonderful, schizophrenic mixture of logic and intuition, that permitted the scientist to run with the logic and then somehow to leap ahead with intuition to places people had never gone before. "INTJ." Introversion, Intuition, Thinking, Judgment. That seemed like Jennifer. At least, it represented her intellectual side. The emotional side remained a mystery he wanted to solve.

"That's what you plan to do, isn't it?"

"Huh?"

"Sometimes I wonder where your mind goes when it wanders off like that. But you know what I'm asking. So tell me right now, or you can forget about your plan."

"Please hear me out on this, OK?"

She folded her arms and leaned into the cave wall. "All right. I'm listening."

Sure she's listening.

He took a deep breath. "I know this mountain like I know the palm of my hand. No, even better than the palm of my hand. There is a way to get us out of here safely."

Her arms remained folded. "OK, what's my part? Out with it before I change my mind."

Before she changes her mind?

Had he actually gained a concession from Jennifer? If so, it might be one that saved their lives.

"OK, first you have to climb the remaining twenty-five feet to the hole in the chimney. I'll be with you each step of the short—"

Her arms unfolded and she clutched the wall. "You mean this nearly one-hundred-feet-above-the-cave-floor climb?"

"You already climbed about three-fourths of it. You know you can do this."

Jennifer took a breath and blew it back out. "OK. Once we're on top, what then?"

"The biggest danger once we're out of the cave is they might get a clear shot at us if they're not in the caves." He illustrated his point with animated hand gestures. "If they come over the ridge top shortly after we exit the chimney we could also be in danger."

"Lee, please don't do that with your hands. Hold onto something. And can we please eliminate that clear-shot danger?"

He decided to hold onto her shoulder. "The best thing we can do to eliminate it is to go now." She didn't seem to mind, so he continued. "They're still in the caves, probably in the same cave system where they nearly found us. If they are in or around any of the caves they're on the wrong side of the ridge to see us."

She removed his hand from her shoulder. "So you're proposing that we crawl out the chimney top, and then run like heck down the other side of the mountain? That's the plan?"

"Something like that." It felt like he was losing the battle on all fronts. "Please hear me out before you comment. Please, Jenn. I thought this through several times and it's the safest and best way to go."

"OK. I'm pretty sure where you're going. Go ahead, finish."

"When we crawl out of the chimney we'll both look carefully to make sure they aren't near the top of the ridge. I know a lookout spot near where we're exiting. We can use it for surveillance—to be sure they can't see us over the ridge top and to make sure they won't get to the ridge top in time to stop us."

"You mean in time to shoot us with that flying-dirt machine gun." Jennifer's face contorted into an expression that hurt him as much as it apparently hurt her.

Is she going to start crying?

The stabbing pain in his gut returned. "I didn't think you saw that. You were completely exhausted."

"I saw enough to know what they were doing and what you did." Her arms encircled his neck before he could react. She leaned into the wall, drew him close, and squeezed hard. Choking back sobs. When the sobs subsided she stepped away and withdrew her arms.

So tender and weak, yet so strong.

He still had a lot to learn about this incredible woman and he wouldn't tolerate further interference from the disparaging thoughts coming from the left side of his brain. Learning all about Jennifer was something he now wanted to do more than anything life on earth offered him.

So, where did Lee Brandt stand right now? Fifty feet up on a cavern wall being hunted by terrorists. That was the good news. A moment ago, he murdered the left side of his brain for blaspheming Jennifer. Before that, he told her he cared for her personally. The only thing he left out was how deeply he cared. Well, that's where he stood, Lee Brandt, a sorry male member of the human species.

Her index finger touched his nose. "You did it again, Lee. It's becoming obvious where you go. Shall I tell you?"

"No, Jenn."

She knew all right, but she wasn't frowning.

That was encouraging.

But right now, he needed to flesh out his plan or he might die a sorry example of a human male.

"So, here's what we need you to do. When we climb out I'll show you an old logging road. It will take you down the backside of this ridge to some houses."

"I haven't heard about anything taking you anywhere." She stared into his eyes.

He ignored the comment, not the eyes. "A few years ago this would have been at least a mile run to the houses. But with all of the new development in the area it's probably more like one-half mile downhill all the way. Can you handle that—two laps around the track, all downhill?"

"I can handle it. What do you have to handle, Lee?"

Jennifer wasn't going to be happy about him staying behind for any reason, or for any length of time.

He needed to be convincing.

They didn't have time to argue.

"The part I have to handle can only be a one-man job. It requires intimacy with this mountain."

She leaned against the cave wall with folded arms again. "I've had some of that over the last few hours. But, mountain man, what else does it require? For you to get shot so I can get away?"

"No. But I won't lie to you. There is some risk, but much less than the risks we've already taken. And when it works I can easily join you while the bad guys are so occupied up here on the mountain the police can just walk up and arrest them."

Jennifer's frown tightened into a scowl. "Lee, that's the biggest bunch of baloney anyone has ever tried to feed—"

"It's not baloney. It's justice for the goons and freedom for us all rolled up into one."

"But, you're not going to tell me—"

"Jenn, I don't like buts."

"But the goons—"

"I really don't like buts, especially theirs. Which, by the way, I have plans for."

Jennifer closed her mouth, pursing her lips.

He doubted her silence came from an appreciation of his pun. Most likely it was to regroup and attack again.

Unexpectedly, mysteriously, her expression mellowed. "If I agree to this you've got to promise me you won't take any chances. Promise me you'll do quickly whatever male pride thing you have planned and then run down this mountain to meet me."

"I promise. And I've got some good reasons for keeping my promise." He tried his most convincing smile, hoping she could see it in the light from the crack in the chimney.

For the first time Jennifer had cut him some slack on something she disagreed with. What did that mean?

"Will you do one more thing for me?" She leaned close to him.

"If I can you know I will."

"Pray for us before we start. Pray hard, if that sort of thing isn't being presumptuous with God."

"I will and it isn't." And Lee did pray really hard.

When he finished and raised his head Jennifer put a hand on each side of his face forcing him to look into her eyes. The dim light exaggerated the size of her brown eyes.

The intense lock was gone. Her gaze looked warm

and inviting.

"Thanks. Now I hope I'm not being presumptuous." She pulled Lee's head down until their lips met. The kiss she gave him was warm and full of promise. As kisses went it was a short one. Coming from Jennifer it was long on meaning.

She pulled her head back a few inches and peered deeply into his eyes. It seemed as if she read all of his thoughts and emotions. This time he masked nothing, allowing her to find whatever she looked for.

When she was through inspecting his soul she smiled. Leaving him no time to savor the moment, she pushed him out onto the cavern wall and took two steps up.

"Let's roll."

13

For the first time in several hours their world grew light as Lee and Jennifer approached the hole at the top of the chimney.

Lee tugged on Jennifer's leg and she stopped climbing while he studied the chimney wall above them looking for a way out through the crack in the rock.

He sighed in relief. "Thank you, Lord. Jenn, the opening's accessible from the wall we're climbing."

Jennifer looked down into his face from her perch above him. "You prayed, Lee. What did you expect?"

"What if we climbed the wrong wall and couldn't reach the opening? You know God doesn't rearrange the world for us each time we pray."

He looked at her face, a dark oval against the sunlight pouring in through the crack.

"Wait a minute. Are we talking about that infinite God of yours? Wouldn't He have known about your prayer before you prayed it? Couldn't He have chased us up the right wall?"

"Oh, me of little faith." He climbed beside Jennifer and stopped. "Yeah. He can do that."

He looked at her and saw Jennifer's face in full sunlight less than three feet from his.

She was breathing deeply. Her cheeks were flushed from the climb and her hair danced with each puff of breeze from above.

He gasped.

"Lee, what's wrong?" She looked at him staring at her. "Oh." Her flushed cheeks turned a deeper shade of red. She looked away.

When she looked back at him, he tried to give her his warmest smile. "Oh...my sentiments exactly." He paused. "Now I'm going to check out our escape hatch. Watch closely how I wedge my body between the two walls. It's called jamming. When I get to the top I'll make sure the area is clear. If there's no sign of anyone I'll climb back down. When we both go up I'll be right behind you. We'll finally complete this climb we started who knows how long ago."

When he turned to climb to the top, Jennifer whispered behind him, "However long ago, it was worth it for me to see the light."

As Lee wedged his body in the crack of the rock, Jennifer's words wedged their way deeply into his mind. Why did this woman always use phrases having double meanings? And what did she really mean when she said "light?"

His train of thought jumped the tracks when his head popped out of the chimney. Temporarily blinded by the bright world of a sunny, mid-March afternoon, he pictured his pupils shrinking to pinpoints when the sunlight hit his eyes. After a second or two in the light, he could no longer see Jennifer in the semi-darkness below. Looking into the daylight again he carefully scanned a complete circle around his position and then stuck his head down into the crack in the rock. "No one in sight, Jenn. Have you heard anything from the cave?"

"Not a sound."

"OK. Make some room. I'm coming down."

Climbing down proved trickier than ascending. His eyes had adjusted to the sunlight so he could see nothing below him. Feeling his way down to the ledge where Jennifer stood he stepped onto it and slid over to the far side to give her climbing room.

"Jenn, just give me a second for my eyes to adjust, and then we'll go up where we can both see the light." He watched to gauge her response.

It was only fair that she wrestle with some double meanings, too.

She avoided his gaze. "What I said, you mean, but, Lee, I didn't..."

Lee let her stumble for a few seconds. He thoroughly enjoyed her discombobulation. Perhaps he enjoyed it because it was a rare event. Or maybe because he enjoyed everything about Jennifer. He put his hand on her shoulder. "You know something, Jenn?" He didn't wait for a reply. "I don't think either one of us could survive an Alaskan winter. Think about it—three months without light. Three hours in a cave and I'm already starved for sunlight. Let's go get some together."

Jennifer eyed the gap above her with a serious frown. But she started climbing into the base of the crack.

He looked up at her silhouette. "Jam your body in like I did. I'll be jammed in right below you each time you take a step. You can't fall."

"You'd better be right about that, Lee, or I'll kill you."

Double meanings. This woman is full of them.

Jennifer worked her way up the crack in the chimney with no problems. After slowly raising her body out of the opening in the huge rock she swept her gaze over the entire panorama. She shielded her eyes with one hand when she looked westward into the sun. "It's still clear."

"Good. Wait for me and then we can work our way over to the lookout point."

A few seconds later they crouched in a small depression near the top of the towering peak. They raised their heads and he pointed to the lookout point thirty yards to the west at the very pinnacle of the spire.

"C'mon, Jenn," he whispered. "Try to keep low and be as quiet as possible."

Like the prolonged darkness in the cave, whispering had started to grate on Lee's nerves. He wanted to use the full range of his vocal expression because there were things he wanted to tell Jennifer for which a whisper was completely inadequate—things where even his words might prove to be inadequate. *But first, I need to carry out this plan.*

Jennifer gasped and closed her eyes when they reach the lookout point. "I can't look down."

He forgot to tell her they would be perched on the very edge of a sheer three-hundred-foot cliff, the north face of the limestone spire.

"Jenn, open your eyes or you really might fall."

Her eyes popped open.

"Slip your legs in here." He pointed to a narrow crack in the rock about two feet from the edge of the cliff. "It's just big enough to jam your legs into up to your thighs, or in your case, to your waist."

After Jennifer dropped into the crack Lee slipped in beside her and gestured towards the open space in front of them. "My buddy and I used to fly paper airplanes off this rock. We had to lean over the edge to launch them." He leaned forward to demonstrate. "See, it's impossible to fall from here with your legs stuck—"

"Please don't do that." She grabbed his jacket and pulled him back.

"Sorry. But look, you can see all of the limestone formation and most of the entire river valley. Look over there." He pointed down to their right. "No, a little more to your right. That's your car and there's the SUV."

"Lee, can't we just—"

"Don't even think about it." He read the urge in Jennifer's eyes and face. "If we make a run for your car we wouldn't make it halfway down before they shot us."

"But it's right there, Lee." Her eyes and voice pleaded as she pointed at her car.

"So close, yet so far away, huh? Well it's only little further down the other side of the mountain to houses, people, and safety."

"I know you're right, but I'm getting impulses to run down to my car."

"Like dangling a carrot in front of—" He'd painted himself into a corner with his simile.

Jennifer rescued him. "Like a chocoholic with a chocolate truffle dangling in front of her."

Lee put his hand on her cheek and gently turned her head away from her car. "Think about it, Jenn. What if somehow we did make it? We would end up in another chase just like last night."

Jennifer placed her fingers over Lee's on her cheek. She squeezed his hand and met his gaze with her intense, brown eyes. "I'm sorry, Lee. I know we can't go down there now and there's no way I want to risk a repeat last night. When you see it in the movies it's all action and adventure. When you live it, it's nothing but panic, terror, and hyperventilation." Jennifer sighed. "So, where is this path you want me to take down the back side of the mountain?"

She still held his hand when he slipped from the crack in the rock. He took her other hand and pulled her out, setting her down a few feet back from the precipice.

"Over here." He continued holding one of her hands and led her between two boulders. They circled a big rock on their right and stopped behind it well-hidden from sight.

"See the old logging road? Look a little to our left and down about two hundred yards."

"I see it. After the big turn it runs almost straight down the side of the mountain."

"That's the idea. Actually, the same road passes near where we're standing. If you go about thirty yards straight through the trees ahead of us you'll find it. It will take you all the way back to civilization."

"I hope so. The people up here are too uncivilized for me. Well, except for one." Jennifer glanced at him.

"And that person is just about to become very uncivilized, too. At least to some spies, terrorists, or whoever these goons really are. When you reach the first house don't stop unless there aren't any other houses nearby. Go on to the second or third house before you knock on any doors. When you call the police remember to tell them the cars are on Holten Creek Road."

Jennifer squinted and frowned, forming what Lee now recognized as her curious face. "Why the second, or third house?"

"There are a few survivalist types around here.

Usually they prefer the end of the road—the highest house on the mountain. After escaping the goons we can't have some American citizen with an overactive imagination shooting at you, can we?"

"I'm not big on irony, Lee."

"Neither am I." He paused. "Are you ready to do this?"

"Only if you follow my rules. Don't take any chances and please come down to me quickly."

"You got it."

"You better have it. Because if you misbehave I can really get you in trouble with NSA. It would be Leavenworth for life, buddy. You got it?"

"I do."

Jennifer smiled briefly, but the smile was cut short by a frown—one he suspected wasn't going away until they were both safely off the mountain. Another reason his plan must succeed.

"I'm going back to the top now, Jenn. If you stand where you are I'll be able to see you. When I'm certain the goons aren't anywhere near the top I'll signal. Then you move straight ahead to the road and run like the wind. But watch the road surface. We can't have you twisting an ankle."

She didn't reply, but she stepped closer to him.

The pain on her drawn face and in her eyes ripped at his heart.

If he didn't go now he might not be able to. He pulled his gaze from the beautiful face and the eyes so deep he feared he might drown in them. He looked at the ground. "When you see me on top, wait for my signal. Godspeed, Jenn."

As Lee turned to climb back to the top two arms encircled his neck, nearly choking him in a fierce hug.

Then they were gone.

The range and intensity of emotions he felt as Jennifer left were impossible to describe with words. In the end, only one emotion remained. Deep determination—a determination to see this plan through.

From the top of the spire he surveyed the entire area around the limestone formations. He raised his hand to give Jennifer the signal to go, but noises came from one of the caves located at the base of the rock.

This was good. Not ideal, but nevertheless good. Though the goons weren't deep inside the rock he knew for certain where they were. From there they could never get to Jennifer if she left now. He gave her the down-the-mountain signal and she disappeared into the trees.

Before launching the second part of the plan—the part he hadn't completely disclosed to her, Lee wanted to see her running far down the road. He needed to be certain she was out of danger.

He stood at the vantage point and waited. In less than a minute she appeared nearly two hundred yards down the road and in a few more seconds she rounded the switchback. When she started down the steep slope Jennifer ran like she was coasting, using gravity to propel her. And she ran like the wind.

"Smart woman," He whispered, smiling at his understatement.

Lee looked upward into the blue sky. "Jenn's away safely. Thank You." He turned his attention to the work at hand. Building a goon trap.

14

Jennifer maneuvered carefully through the trees avoiding twigs that might snap and other noisy blunders. When she stepped between two small trees and pushed aside some branches the road lay at her feet.

The road would lead her down the mountain for help, but her heart pulled her in the opposite direction, back to help Lee. But going back might endanger him so she would keep her promise.

"Please, God, protect him," she whispered as she stepped onto the old logging road.

This is becoming a habit.

Was her new habit born of desperation or a growing faith? Unsure of the answer she deferred the question until later.

Jennifer started jogging slowly, letting her leg muscles warm up. Soon she had stretched out the kinks from the hours spent hiding in the cave. Her muscles warmed and relaxed. But not her mind. It couldn't stop worrying about Lee.

I know he's intelligent and he knows these mountains, but please keep him safe.

Another prayer. Desperation or faith? The question remained. So would her spontaneous prayers…at least for now.

After Jennifer passed the saddle between two peaks she reached the switchback where the road turned to the right and then plunged downward in a steep descent to the valley floor. Gravity wanted to take over now, and she gave in to its force, for speed and to conserve energy. As she accelerated Jennifer used her leg strength to hold back so she wouldn't lose control of her body.

The road steepened and she felt like she was flying down the mountain. The feeling was so exhilarating she couldn't resist letting gravity have its way. She had never gotten into running. But if it could give her this sensation she vowed to begin running every day.

She flew down the mountain for another two-hundred yards. Over the treetops a whole residential development appeared. Those houses were a considerable distance from the mountain.

Another hundred yards down the road, she passed the upper end of a mountainside meadow. The new spring grass was a brilliant green and the early wildflowers sprinkled it with yellow and lavender. At the base of the meadow lay house number one.

The long wait to call for help—the wait filled with one frustration after another—was nearly over.

Jennifer felt an urge to run straight to the door of the house. As her gaze swept the property it settled on the driveway. A large iron gate blocked access to the house. She looked on both sides of the gate. The owner had fenced the entire property.

A survivalist?

She'd heard of those who so distrusted the government and nearly everyone else that they fortified themselves in their houses. She saw some of their websites filled with conspiracy theories. Theories such as 9-11 being an "inside job." Her time with NSA provided access to facts proving the foolishness of such thought.

She had analyzed some of the 9-11 terrorists' communications, gleaning intelligence NSA could not obtain until after the attack. What she learned about the evil behind the attacks motivated her to undertake her current work developing tools to thwart terrorist plots.

Another two hundred yards would take her to house number two, which sat close beside houses number three and four. Beyond those houses there were many more. These were the homes of people who did not shrink from community. She made her choice—house number two as Lee recommended.

Thoughts of myriad different possibilities ran through her mind as she ran to the front door. But Lee said he "prayed hard" and she saw enough in the last twenty-four hours to believe God answered. The God she doubted for the past two years—the years since her father died.

She pushed the doorbell button.

Please, let the right person answer.

A peace swept over her. She was meant to be standing in front of this house at this very time. Somehow, she was certain.

The door opened a crack at first, then all the way. A graying, middle-aged lady cocked her head and frowned. "Can I help you, miss?"

"Ma'am, my name is Jennifer Akihara and my friend is in trouble on the mountain." Jennifer gestured towards the peak she hoped Lee would run down in a few minutes.

The woman cocked her head to the other side. She studied Jennifer for a couple of seconds. "I know you. You're the young lady who is missing—I guess I should say *was* missing. Come in. Come in. My name is Marie Benson and you probably want to use the phone."

Puzzled by being recognized so quickly, Jennifer hesitated before entering. After the car bombing, the shooting, and two people missing, her picture and Lee's were probably in the Saturday paper and shown on TV. Good. That meant the police and the FBI were searching for them.

"Miss, are you coming in?"

I've got to get focused.

"Yes, ma'am. I need to talk to the police. My friend could be killed and we might possibly be in danger here."

"My goodness, here's the phone. Call. Oh yes, you'll need to tell them our address. It's 4504 West Marie Street."

Jennifer stepped to the phone and dialed. The 911 operator came on the line and immediately recognized her name.

After the operator obtained the preliminary information things began to move quickly. "The Kerbyville police are on the way. They should be at the Benson's house in three or four minutes."

She sighed. "Good. Please tell them the people who chased us have automatic weapons—more than one—maybe two or three. Also tell them Lee Brandt is still on the mountain trying to elude the gunmen and then join me down here."

"Thank you. I'll pass your information to Officer Robbins." After a short pause, the operator was back. "Is there anything else the police should know?"

"Yes. As far as I know, the gunmen are still on the mountain. They may be held up there for a while if

Lee's plan is successful. But my car, a white, older sedan, is about a mile or two up Holten Creek Road below the limestone spire. The gunmen's car is a black SUV. It will be parked nearby if they're still on the mountain."

"Thanks again. I will pass the information to them in just a moment. You should be hearing sirens, now."

"Yes, I hear them."

"Good. Now I want to alert you to what will likely happen next—it could get a little crazy where you are. First, the local police will arrive. But we think the media might arrive about the same time. Your story is a hot news item. If a media circus starts, avoid them and talk only to the police. And I've been told that soon some folks other than the police will be there to talk with you. I thought you should know."

Jennifer could guess who "some people" would be, some members of the JTTF and, not long after, an NSA agent.

"Officer Robbins is out front, now. Good luck. We're glad you're safe and thanks for the information you provided."

Jennifer hung up and hurried to the door with Mrs. Benson trailing behind her. She pulled the door open and looked up into the kindly face of the biggest policeman she'd ever seen.

"Ms. Akihara, I'm Officer Robbins. Let's sit down and you can give me the information you have and I'll call it in. Then I'll tell you what I know and we can proceed from there."

Maybe this was the end of this dreadful drama. Perhaps it was the beginning of a much better one, provided Lee made it safely down the mountain.

Please, God, help him.

15

Retribution. It was the word of the hour.

Lee anticipated it like a forehand kill shot on a racquetball court. He hadn't lied when he said his plan wasn't about sacrificing himself so she could get away. However, if the goons came over the ridge line in the next couple of minutes he would draw attention to himself and away from Jennifer, gladly taking any associated risks.

He waited for two minutes. No goons. He would now draw their attention to something else, something of his choosing.

Over the backside of the ridgeline from the goons Lee ran to reach another limestone outcropping three hundred yards to the southeast. There, a large cave ran the full length of the big rock, a distance of nearly one hundred yards. Halfway in a dogleg hid the far end of the cave from anyone who entered.

Upon entering this cave it took several seconds for the human eye to adjust. Initially, only the largest features of the cave were visible. That's what he needed to pull off this part of his plan—the initial inability to see the details. In this cave, at this particular time, the devil really was in the details. The thought brought a smile to his face as he ran.

Nineteen years ago Lee and his buddy became intimately, and most unpleasantly, acquainted with a phenomenon occurring in the cave in mid-March after a cold winter.

Last winter was cold and snowy, typical of La Nina winters in the Pacific Northwest. What he needed to know today was whether the timing was right for the effects he counted on. Bad timing would convert the trap to nothing more than a short detour. If that happened he could end up in a desperate run for his life.

He loped through the fir trees and scrubby oaks growing on the south side of the ridge. After a couple of minutes he approached the east end of the long cave. When he reached the top of a small rise he walked cautiously towards the cave's mouth. It wouldn't do to walk in on a mama black bear with cubs. Being killed by a bear instead of an assault rifle would be worse than ironic.

He slipped to the right side of the cave's east entrance and rolled up his left shirt sleeve. He wouldn't expose his injured right arm to the abuse he anticipated. He hugged the rock forming the face of the cave, gritted his teeth and plunged his bare arm into the darkness. After waiting a full second he pulled his arm out and backpedaled rapidly away from the opening.

He brushed his hand and arm furiously to remove every trace of the blackness covering them. A wide grin spread across his face. The timing was perfect.

The winter weather had been miserable, but as Lee set his snare for the goons, he thanked God for every cold, snowy day. Treading lightly he backtracked towards the spire, staying two hundred yards off to the side of the trail. He didn't want to leave any tracks pointing back to the limestone spire so he kept to the rocks as much as possible.

Near the spire he stopped and listened for the goons. No sounds. Nothing.

Running so as to leave behind fresh tracks and broken earth, he returned to the cave. He looked back towards the spire. His tracks left a clear trail. Satisfied with his work he returned to the pinnacle of the spire once again using the rocks to the side of the trail to hide his tracks.

Two dicey parts to his scheme remained. The first required getting the goons attention without giving them a clear shot at him. He hadn't disclosed this part to Jennifer. She would have said—he didn't even want to think about the threats she would have made.

The second part, the diciest one, required luring the goons to the trail of tracks so they would follow it one-quarter mile to the other cave. While the goons followed his trail he must remain far ahead of them and out of sight or—he didn't want to think about that consequence, either.

He moved to a boulder on the west edge of the spire and studied the slope below him for a few moments. Below his position slide areas lay scattered around the limestone formation. An abundance of limestone chunks lay on the steep slope and each chunk possessed enough potential energy to participate in his scheme. The rocks needed a little shove, a kick, or perhaps another rock tossed onto them to release their kinetic state.

When two of the goons emerged from the large cave at the base of the rock nearly three-hundred feet below him he stepped from behind the boulder.

They were engaged in an animated hand-waving conversation and they didn't look up towards him. He selected a softball-sized rock and moved out onto the shoulder of the spire. The spot featured a fairly easy, though very long, climb up from the base. It was the shortest path to his location. The goons would take it.

Lee stepped from behind the shoulder of the rock and tossed his chunk of limestone onto a small slide area below him. He turned around to make it appear he was climbing up the rock to escape.

Small at first, the slide soon became an impressive avalanche. Maybe they would think he was trying to take them out with a rock slide. That a weaponless man would even attempt to take them out might enrage them. Anger would fuel their desire to follow him while blunting their suspicion.

Lee turned his head and glanced down towards the goons. The avalanche missed them by a few yards, but their gaze followed the slide up to its origin. Two sets of eyes were looking directly at him.

He took several steps in the direction he wanted them to follow and then cut behind a boulder. When he topped the ridge his last view of the goons was indelibly stamped on his memory. They had raised their weapons to shoot.

By keeping the ridge between them for the next minute he would remain out of their sight while he ran along the trail of tracks leading to the destination cave — the cave of destiny.

Good name. The cave of destiny.

As he sprinted down the backside of the mountain, Lee put the sequence of events working out behind him in fast forward, playing them like a video in his mind.

The goons would take a minute or more to climb up the steep slope. They would stop for a few seconds to catch their breath and then look in the direction he had gone.

There his tracks began. By then he would have tripled his lead, keeping him far out of sight, out of earshot, and out of shooting range.

Unless he fell and injured himself he was home free. He would soon see Jennifer.

But there's something else I need to see first.

Moving through the trees towards the cave of destiny he had, at most, sixty seconds to hide himself. After running nearly one hundred yards he leaped off the trail and onto a stretch of bare limestone rock protruding up from the mountain's back side. This vein of limestone ran for a considerable distance perpendicular to his tracks and towards a saddle located between the limestone spire and a smaller peak to the southwest. He would hide at the saddle.

In less than thirty seconds, trees hid him and he was nearly half way to his camouflaged hiding place in the saddle. The saddle lay nearly one-quarter mile from the cave of destiny, two hundred feet higher and nearly one-quarter mile closer to Jennifer and safety. It provided a view of the area near the opening of the cave.

While he scampered towards his hiding place he recalculated the amount of time he gave Jennifer to summon the police. If this plan failed he might be leading the goons down to houses where innocent people resided.

She had at least thirty minutes already, but it should take only five or ten minutes to summon the police. The events of last night undoubtedly resulted in every patrolman in the state looking for Jennifer, him, and a bunch of gunmen.

Lee put that worry out of his mind, but another

worry quickly replaced it.

Jennifer was going to be concerned.

No. That's a euphemism.

She would be furious when he arrived. She didn't expect him to take this long—not nearly this long and he had made a promise to her.

He held onto one hope. When he told her what he did to the goons maybe she would forgive him. He'd seen enough to know forgiveness was not a certainty. Would their kiss in the cave help his cause?

The more he thought about it, his plan smacked of masculine pride. That fact might make her even angrier. If he pulled this off he would have a story a guy could tell his kids and his grandkids. But if Jennifer didn't forgive him he might be telling his story to fellow convicts in Leavenworth.

Lee skirted the clearing below the saddle and settled into his observation point. As soon as they topped the ridge the goons found his tracks and headed down the trail. They moved quickly, but they were being cautious.

At this rate they would reach the cave in about three minutes. He started timing them with the second hand on his watch. At two minutes and forty-five seconds three goons emerged from the trees and stood in front of the rise leading up to the cave's mouth. All three carried assault rifles.

The three spread out in a single row. Shoulder-to-shoulder they walked slowly up the slope. When they topped the rise and saw the mouth of the cave they stopped abruptly.

He chuckled.

They probably weren't excited about any more spelunking adventures. But the trail was hot and he watched as they entered the wide mouth of the cave three abreast.

He knew what would happen next. Lee and his buddy entered similarly nineteen years ago. They never went near that cave again in the spring.

A loud shriek came from the cave far below.

He couldn't stifle his laughter. He didn't need to.

The screams of the three goons became too loud for them to hear anything but each other.

While he convulsed with belly-shaking laughter, the goons repeatedly yelled two words, "*awrah*" and "*haraam.*" He seemed to recall from his study of Islam, that the words meant something like nakedness and forbidden.

Lee remembered how it was for him when the screaming started. His exposed skin began itching and burning within a second. His entire form became black, coated with evil, crawling, hopping fleas—fleas left by hibernating bears two or three weeks earlier.

After the bears left the fleas multiplied without a host until there were millions of ravenous insects desperate for blood. One bite could make a person wince and scratch. Multiply it by ten thousand and the pain became unbearable. Clothing did nothing to stop the fleas' inexorable conquest of every square inch of skin on the human body.

He had felt contaminated, beyond any hope of being clean again, and he worried about dread diseases the little pests sometimes carried.

The three goons ran from the cave littering the ground behind them with their clothing. They weren't carrying their guns. This was better than he hoped for. They had dropped their weapons in the cave after they were shrink-wrapped in fleas.

A shrill scream pierced his ears.

Was one of the goons a gooness?

He moved to his right around a small pond fed by an underground spring. After jumping down an embankment and onto the road he began his run. He ran to set a world record in the downhill eight hundred meters—running towards civilized people, the police, safety, and Jennifer.

As he ran a question crossed his mind. Would the goons go back into the cave to get their guns? No way this side of...well...this side of the place the goons felt they were in.

16

Standing in the Benson's backyard near the shop, the makeshift command post, Jennifer stewed, worried, and stewed some more. Lee promised he would complete his plan and be here shortly after she arrived.

What does shortly mean? Ten minutes? Fifteen?

It had been forty-five minutes since Jennifer started her run down the mountain. He should have been here thirty minutes ago. A lot could happen in thirty minutes. Too much.

Everything Jennifer thought and felt in those last few minutes with Lee came rushing back to her mind and heart. Despite the attack on them it wasn't supposed to be like this. What had happened to the Jennifer Akihara she knew so well? Where was the woman who only wanted to protect herself from men—the woman who would never pray? Maybe the goons really did kill someone Friday night, the old Jennifer. In her place was a woman Lee called Jenn. But she could only be Jenn if Lee made it safely down the mountain.

Would this God she recently became aware of permit her to lose another person she cared for as He did with her father? Wrestling with that question brought Lee's prayer to mind, the one he prayed before they left the cave.

God could take care of Lee. She believed that.

But what if Lee doesn't take care of Lee? What if he took

too many chances?

When Jennifer's thoughts intensified they became furious words and emotions which she vented. "If God comes through for him, maybe He's a God I can trust. But I'm going to kill Lee when he gets down here, anyway. I'm going to kill him!"

Officer Robbins rounded the corner of the house and clutched her shoulders to prevent a collision. "You do that, young lady, and I'll have to arrest you."

There was authority in his voice, but a wide grin on his face.

She closed her eyes and dropped her head. Her cheeks were hot. Probably glowing red.

What happened to Jennifer Akihara? Will someone please tell me?

H. L. Wegley

17

As Lee ran from his camouflaged hiding place on the saddle, the shouts and shrieks of the goons echoed between the two peaks. He turned his head towards the cave of destiny and spoke some encouragement.

"Eat'em alive, guys."

The fleas, by their very nature, would do their best to comply. Now it was time to go plead his case with Jennifer.

When Lee broke into an all out sprint he let gravity share in the process. The joy of a mission completed and thoughts of the person waiting for him gave him a surge of energy.

Ninety seconds later Lee stood in front of house number two, hands on hips and out of breath. This had to be the place. It looked like center ring in a three-ring circus.

Jennifer seemed to stir things up wherever she went.

He scanned the array of vehicles and equipment around him for a few seconds. Thankfully, there were enough police cars to deter the gunmen even if they were miraculously delivered from the fleas.

The safety issue settled; he began looking for Jennifer. As he stood repaying his oxygen debt a middle-aged man approached.

"You must be Lee Brandt. Half the county and a certain young lady have been waiting for you. I know, because I've been watching it on TV. Hi. I'm Walt Benson."

"Mr. Benson, you mean all those vans—"

"Yep. Media mania. All have cameras rolling right now. Probably trained on us."

Lee cocked his head and frowned. "But why isn't Jennifer here?"

Mr. Benson raised his fist and pointed his thumb behind him. "The police set up temporary headquarters out back in my shop out of reach of the media. I've heard some folks from the metropolitan area JTTF are on their way here now. You'll be meeting with them in my shop."

Lee heard a familiar voice. It wasn't whispering.

"I don't care. I'm going out there, anyway."

He turned towards the voice.

Jennifer strode around the corner of the house. Her furious pace apparently reflected her mood.

He braced himself for the verbal barrage.

It came when she broke into a run fifteen yards away. "Lee Brandt, I'm going to kill you!" Jennifer yelled, causing every head within two hundred yards to turn towards her. She smashed into Lee, still yelling. "Don't ever lie to me again!"

He stepped backward.

This is gonna be worse than I anticipated.

How could he defuse Jennifer?

Before he found an appropriate reply Jennifer drew her hand back. She was going to slap his face to the next county.

Her words stopped. She dropped her hand. Tears began to flow.

I hate it when women do that.

Mostly he hated the pain their tears inflicted. But

this time the pain prompted an impulse. He wasn't sure what would happen if he acted on his feelings, but whatever the price, holding Jennifer seemed worth it. If it required running to the next county to retrieve his face, so be it. He stepped forward wrapping his arms around her, embracing both her and the reality that they were together, alive, and safe.

As they stood on the Benson's front lawn, a huddle of two, he wanted to console her. "Jenn I've got some good news, our—"

"There can't be any good news now." More tears streaked her face.

He pulled her head against his cheek and spoke softly. "What do you mean, can't be any good news?"

She put her arms around him hiding her face in his chest. "I've just made a complete fool of myself in front of the entire world."

He looked up at the five or six media vans along the street. Each video camera was pointed at Jennifer and him. He was afraid to agree with her statement, but he knew better than to disagree. "Oh, boy, we're never going to live this down."

"See what I mean?" Jennifer sobbed, looking up at him.

He looked down into her face. It was a perfect face and the perfect moment. "Do you really want me to tell you what I see?"

"No, Lee...not here." Jennifer said the words, but she offered no resistance.

At the upturned face, he could think of nothing else to do but to kiss her—long and shamelessly—in front of the entire world. While he did, the cameras continued to roll.

When their lips separated he was the one who

pulled back. "I thought you wanted to kill me."

She rested her cheek on his shoulder. "I still do. But I can wait a few minutes."

18

Lee and Jennifer looked up at the sound of people shouting. All around the three-ring circus, people clapped and voiced their approval—everyone except the cameramen, who were too busy shooting video.

Lee knew he would have questions to answer at his next men's accountability meeting. He didn't care. The kiss was worth it.

Thankfully, their position at center ring was short-lived.

A black sedan pulled in front of the Benson's house and the crowd buzzed when two men in suits emerged. The two walked straight towards Jennifer and him as they stood arm-in-arm on the lawn.

The tall man spoke first. "Hello, I'm Agent Peterson, FBI. This is my assistant, Agent Bastian."

"I'm Lee Brandt and this is Jennifer Akihara."

The assistant stepped in front of the main man, Peterson. Not a good thing to do.

"Ms. Akahari, good to meet you." His gaze, lingered on Jennifer longer than Lee thought appropriate, and then Bastian dismissed her and turned towards him. "Lee, where can we get some privacy?"

Wherever they found this guy...they need to stop looking there.

He stared into the man's eyes. "Her name is Akihara, Jennifer Akihara. Ms. Akihara has made arrangements with Officer Robbins of the Kerbyville police to use the shop behind the Bensons' house for us to 'get some privacy'."

Peterson scowled. But, for the moment, he seemed to be watching his underling like he was feeding him rope.

Lee squeezed Jennifer's hand hoping she understood that he wanted to deal with this guy.

She gave Lee a squinting frown then a nod.

Good. Rather than wait for an opportunity he would create one. "Why don't you show our FBI friends the area you and Officer Robbins set up."

"We should keep the group down to a minimum—just those who know and those who need to know. So, do we really need Miss Aka—uh...Akihara?" Bastian spoke again.

This guy was continuing just like he started, foot in mouth, brains in neutral.

Lee's mouth opened, but Jennifer beat him to the verbal punch. One glance at her cool, staring eyes made it clear. She was primed to deliver a knockout blow. He closed his mouth.

You'd better duck, Bastian.

Jennifer's gaze locked on Bastian's face. "Mr. Bastian, do you sometimes use data and reports from NSA?"

Bastian hesitated and turned towards Peterson. "Peterson, uh...is it OK for me to answer that?"

Jennifer rolled her eyes.

Even Lee knew the fact that the FBI used intelligence reports from NSA was not classified information.

Peterson nodded to Bastian. Peterson covered his mouth with his hand. Was he struggling to keep a straight face, or yawning?

"Yes we do." Bastian replied.

Jennifer's gaze switched to laser mode. "Then you are undoubtedly familiar with my work, if you do read reports and use data provided to you by NSA. My name, again, is Jennifer Akihara."

A question and a statement from Jennifer and Bastian was already backpedaling. "Oh, that Jennifer Akihara."

Lee didn't have a clue whether Bastian had actually read Jennifer's work. But the name evidently clicked with him.

Peterson sighed and stepped in front of his underling. "Jennifer is needed here for several reasons. And, Bastian, she has a higher clearance than you do. Show us the way, Miss Akihara."

When they entered the shop the assortment of equipment indicated this was a large woodshop. In an open area several chairs sat configured in a circle. They each picked a chair and sat down.

Jennifer chose a chair beside Lee. That was a good sign. Maybe the kiss did the trick.

He glanced at her face.

Maybe not.

Officer Robbins came in as they were being seated. "Good to see you, Lee—even better to see you still in one piece."

"Good to see you too, Dan. Jennifer, Dan Robbins is one of the friends on the Kerbyville police force whom I mentioned last night."

"Lee, we met *an hour ago.* You'll never know what a relief it was to meet him."

"Yeah. He was probably the first person you'd seen with a gun since yesterday evening who wasn't pointing it at you."

Jennifer glared at him. Evidently she didn't appreciate his attempt at humor. Maybe Dan would.

He turned his gaze back to Dan. "We tried to make it to Kerbyville before sunrise, Dan, but I thought spending the day in a cave with Jennifer sounded more romantic."

"That's enough, Lee. Climbing a one-hundred foot goo-covered rock wall in the dark is anything but romantic."

"But you gotta' admit, Jenn, the view from the top was worth it." He scanned Jennifer's face—a face hidden from him until it was lit by the opening at the top of the chimney, the place where Jennifer kissed him.

She shot him a frowning glance. "Very funny."

Evidently, she didn't want to be reminded.

Peterson pursed his lips. His face looked like he wanted to pound a gavel and demand for order in the court. He took a calming breath. "Jennifer, just to let you and Lee know, a few minutes ago we received a report from Trooper Brower, who was sent to check out the vehicles."

Her eyes widened. "Was my car OK?"

Peterson nodded. "Yes, but due to unusual circumstances, Brower was forced to stop the SUV by ramming it. Brower is OK, just needed a couple of stitches."

Lee leaned forward towards Peterson. "So you got the goons, right?"

Peterson's eyebrows nearly touched at his question. "We...we got one of them."

Frowning, Lee slid forward in his chair. "Have you gotten anything out of him?"

"Actually, it was a she. Unfortunately...she was dead at the scene. Not from the collision. From a bullet through her head. Evidently the uh...*goons* considered her expendable. The funny thing was...a red rash completely covered her body."

Jennifer's mouth fell open. "You mean one of the goons was a woman?"

The capture of the goons wasn't playing out quite like he had planned. He frowned and shook his head. "What about the others?"

"It appears there were two others. One was apparently injured in the crash. We don't know about the third one. We suspect both are still in the area so we have set up several roadblocks and initiated a large-scale search. We've notified the residents in the area to assume these men are armed and dangerous and to keep their doors locked."

A knock on the door interrupted their conversation.

Peterson answered it.

A hand reached in and gave him a slip of paper. He read it and looked up at his understudy. "Bastian, Agent Stewart from NSA arrived at the Kerbyville police station. I want you to personally escort him here."

"I'm on my way."

When Bastian left, Peterson seemed to relax. He sighed and looked at Lee. "Back to the subject at hand. We recovered one assault rifle from the SUV and a Glock from the lady. But, Lee, you said you saw more weapons."

"Jennifer and I saw at least two automatic weapons when they fired at her car."

At his comment, her head popped up, "Speak for

yourself. Remember who was driving?"

"And driving incredibly," he said. "It's a miracle we escaped them on the freeway." He studied her face, hoping her anger would stop boiling to the surface.

"It was...a miracle." Her voice had softened.

"About the weapons...I saw three assault rifles shortly before I left the mountain to come down here." He had finally steered the conversation to the trap.

Jennifer's head snapped towards him. Her eyes glared. "Lee, you weren't supposed to see any guns—not supposed to be taking chances. You promised you wouldn't do that, remember?"

He thought he had steered the conversation in a better direction.

Maybe his best chance to get back into her good graces was simply to tell the truth about his plan and hope for the best. He tried again to introduce the subject of the trap. "You'll find the unaccounted for weapons in a cave I led them to on this side of the ridge."

Peterson's eyebrows raised, and he cleared his throat. "Please tell me, Lee, why you think these terrorists would abandon their weapons in some cave, especially since they needed them to kill you, and then get away."

On the words "kill you," Jennifer glared at him.

"It's a long story, Peterson, but they had literally a million reasons for leaving their guns behind. It was all part of a plan Jennifer and I—"

Jennifer jumped to her feet. "He's about to tell you the same baloney he told me before he sent me down the mountain and then stayed up there for fun and games." Her voice grew louder. "You can't—"

"All right, you two!" Peterson's gavel came down

hard. "I can see there is something festering just under the surface. But if you'll just stick to communicating the facts for the next few minutes I'll leave you alone shortly to sort out the...uh...other stuff."

"Jenn, Agent Peterson, I need to tell you the part of our plan I...well...didn't fully disclose to Jennifer."

Jennifer's entire body jerked at his last words.

He hurried to make his case before Jennifer could interrupt him. "It was a plan to get Jennifer down here safely and it worked. It could have stopped the goons right there on the mountain. It appears it nearly did."

"I only called it baloney because I can't think of a single thing you could have done to stop the goons and get away, short of magically turning into some superhero." Jennifer spoke softly.

"That's because you didn't grow up with Colby and me."

"With whom?"

At least her tone was civil.

"The buddy I mentioned several times while we were on the mountain. That was Colby. You see, Agent Peterson, we experienced something terrifying up there in mid-March right after a La Nina winter much like the one we just came through. We discovered a cave northeast of the spire and about three hundred yards down the south side of the ridge."

Peterson shuffled his feet and frowned. "Please continue, but spare us the unnecessary details."

He realized he was speaking half to Jennifer and half to Peterson.

Obviously, the tall FBI agent wasn't going to tolerate any more of that.

Lee took a deep breath, exhaled, and rewound his story. "OK. We found a cave where some bears hibernate every winter. After a cold winter like we just came through, they seem to stay in the cave until early March. They leave behind an incredible infestation of fleas. After a couple of weeks of multiplying and not having food, the fleas are ravenous and they number into the millions."

He paused to let the facts sink in. "When my buddy and I walked into the cave in mid-March, about twenty feet in, the fleas all leaped in unison. They completely coated us and nearly ate us alive. When we ran out of the cave we were literally black all over. The pain was unbearable and those little devils just kept penetrating deeper into unbitten territory. We couldn't stop screaming. We had no choice but to shed our clothes and wash the fleas off our bodies in a snow-fed stream. It takes a while. Then we had to shake the fleas out of our clothes before getting dressed. That whole process can take from thirty minutes to an hour. I figured the goons would be held up long enough for Jennifer to tell the police where the cars were and for the police to catch the goons before they could escape."

Peterson frowned and cocked his head. "Did you really believe hardened terrorists would stop to get rid of some fleas?"

"Believe me, Peterson, the pain is unbearable and the feeling of defilement, while it's a psychological thing, is overpowering."

"I'll take your word on that. Apparently it did just that."

"Is that what you meant by intimacy with the mountain?" Jennifer asked.

He nodded.

But was Peterson buying his story?

From his expression Lee couldn't tell.

Peterson sat rubbing his chin. "Now tell us again how you got them to the cave?"

"OK. When Jennifer was well down the road I made some clear tracks leading up to the mouth of the cave. Then I went back to the spire and waited for the goons...and the gooness, to stop looking for Jennifer and me in the caves. When they came out at the base of the spire I started a small rock slide and I let them see me running away towards the tracks leading to the cave."

"You gave them a clear shot at you? You promised not to take any chances!" Jennifer's volume rose.

He desperately needed diminuendo. "I was careful, honest."

Jennifer still glared at him, unappeased.

He cleared his throat and continued. "Well, by the time the goons climbed up to the spire I had already jumped from the trail and hid in a saddle a quarter mile away. From there I could see the cave, but I still had quick access to the old logging road and a short run down to this place." He paused and checked Jennifer's reaction. "The goons took the bait and went into the cave three abreast, each carrying an assault rifle. Within a few seconds there was all kinds of shrieking and screaming coming from the cave. The goons came running out without their guns and without half of their clothes—they ripped the other half off while they ran from the cave."

"You mean you actually pulled that off?" Peterson's brow was furled and his head cocked.

"Lured them into the cave, yes. But they were doing all of the pulling off. That's when I ran down here."

Peterson sat still for moment, processing the story.

Then he began a belly-shaking laugh—a whole series of belly-shaking guffaws.

Jennifer's angry look turned to a smile which grew into a giggle.

Soon, the three of them laughed loud and long.

The remaining tension and anxiety of the previous eighteen hours drained from Jennifer and him, while Peterson acquired a story he would probably enjoy sharing with his cohorts for a long time to come.

When their laughter subsided, he caught his breath. "And so, Agent Peterson, do you think those other guns are still in the cave?"

"I'd bet money on it."

An idea popped into his head. "I noticed that you and Bastian...well...things don't go smoothly when you two work together, do they?"

"When you have a young partner that comes with the territory," Peterson managed between chuckles.

"Well, sir, you could send Bastian up to retrieve the guns." He joked. "But he better wear a hazmat suit."

Peterson shook his head and continued to chuckle.

Lee caught Jennifer looking at him. Her eyes were something less than hostile.

Carpe diem.

"Please forgive me?" He mouthed the words.

She looked away, but her sulky look appeared contrived.

Still chuckling, Peterson stood. "Well, I think we've got enough to go on for now. I'll leave you two here for a bit. When Joe Morrison gets here we'll talk about the computer issues you uncovered."

The moment the door closed behind Peterson, Lee swiveled his chair to face Jennifer. He placed his hand on her cheek and gently turned her face towards him. There was no resistance. He tried to *carpe diem* again. "I'm sorry. I didn't mean to hurt you or deceive you. I just wanted to keep you safe and to make sure the goons would be caught."

Jennifer's gaze bored into him again. "No. That's not all you wanted. Don't lie to me again."

This was not going well, so he decided to do what any red-blooded male would do when a relationship with someone like Jennifer was on the line. "I'll do anything you want—anything for you to forgive me. Just tell me—"

"I liked you better as the tough mountain man— my hero, who saved me from the goons. But you're just...just a...groveling wimp!"

"You know me better than that." He paused and took a calming breath. "Jenn...you're right. I wanted something else, too. For what they did to us I wanted *revenge*. And when the screaming started and their clothes flew off, *I got it*."

Forgive me, Lord...

Jennifer stared into his eyes for several seconds, studying them. There were no traces of anger in her eyes or on her face. "Well, at least you finally told me the truth. But if we're ever in danger again..."

Again? Was she implying there would be an "again" for them?

She sat quietly waiting. "Now that you're back...as I was saying, in the future you'd better spill your guts up front not after the fact. I won't be kept in the dark. Is that understood?"

He struggled hard to suppress a strong urge to wrap his arms around her. "Understood. No secret plans—ever."

Jennifer's eyes softened farther. "There's more here than just me demanding honesty. I don't want to lose anyone I care for again. I've gone through that once and I can't—" She stopped and her mouth closed.

Jennifer said "care for" and placed him in a category with the person she felt closest to, her dad.

"Do you ever again intend to be chased by thugs, shot at, and hide out in caves all night?"

"No, of course not."

"Neither do I. And I promise you, with all those same intentions, I'll never endanger—"

"OK, here's the deal. You break your promise and you have to run the flea cave in your underwear on March 19th." Though her expression contained a smile, the intense stare from those all-knowing brown eyes told him she would hold his feet to the fire on the issue of honesty. She had actually relented.

Forgiven him.

Relief flooded over Lee's tense body and mind. He tried to return her smile. "You sure drive a hard bargain when it comes to forgiveness."

"Am I worth it?" She studied his face.

"Yeah, at least two or three runs through the cave."

Jennifer stood and he followed her cue. She wrapped her arms around him and pressed her cheek into his chest. Her bear hug reminded him of her arm strength when she yanked him into the crevice on the cavern wall. It was long on bear and a little short on hug, but he reveled in it.

"I forgive you, but don't do that to me again. Ever. You have two strikes on you now."

"Jenn, two strikes? Which two?"

"You're a guy and you deceived me."

He hadn't even seen the first pitch and the second was a little outside.

"Howie warned me," he mumbled.

"Howie? I knew it. Do you realize Howie was playing matchmaker Friday night?"

"Was he successful?"

Her only reply was the enigmatic smile.

19

Lee deceived Jennifer and she forgave him. According to Howie this was out of character for her. She had done something extremely difficult for her. That spoke volumes.

He stood looking at this beautiful woman.

The two stood facing each other with both pairs of hands clasped, when the door popped open.

Peterson stuck his head in. "Looks like the...other stuff has been taken care of. Anyone in here need some coffee?" Peterson entered carrying a coffeepot and a package of Styrofoam cups.

Jennifer nodded and grabbed a cup.

He took a cup, too. His anxiety had drained away taking the benefit of adrenaline with it. Any coffee was most welcome. "It's not gourmet coffee, but right now I'll take anything with caffeine in it."

Peterson placed the coffee pot on the workbench lining one side of the room. "Joe Morrison and someone who says he's your boss are on their way here to see you. They should arrive in a few minutes, as will Bastian with Agent Stewart from NSA."

Lee quickly rehearsed the scenario that would soon play out. He stepped close to Jennifer and took her free hand. "You need to know what to expect when my boss and Joe Morrison, the fellow you didn't get to meet yesterday evening, get here."

She dropped his hand. "OK, but is there anything

important you haven't told me?"

Was Jennifer looking for strike three? If he was going down on strikes he would at least go down swinging. "It would have been taken care of when we met with Joe."

"I'm not in any trouble with National Aerospace, am I? You said I could count on you, remember, 'have no fear, Lee is here'?"

But he had fear.

I fear I'm an idiot.

He remembered his words and her reaction to them. "Let me finish first and then the three of us can get consensus on the subject."

She set her coffee cup on the workbench. "You didn't lead me into some bug-infested cave right from the get-go, did you?"

"No, but you know the badge I got for—"

"It didn't authorize me to do much, did it?" Jennifer folded her arms across her chest.

"No. Just visit the facility with me as your escort. It was my decision, and mine alone, to disclose certain information to you. It was also my decision to allow you computer access to gather the intelligence to identify the conspirators. So in theory it's my head on the block, not yours."

Her arms still folded, Jennifer frowned. "In theory, huh. National Aerospace will understand all that and why you brought me into the investigation, won't they?"

Lee followed the negative trend in Jennifer's body language. Her pitch was a wicked slider breaking over the plate. With two strikes he at least had to foul it away. "I didn't follow established protocols for bringing you in. Though we had no direct access to classified or restricted data I'm hoping your clearance through NSA and the NSA agent who's coming will vouch for you and smooth things over with Joe Morrison. Technically, you're cleared for everything but National Aerospace proprietary information. And your need to know—well, that's a matter of interpretation."

Peterson stared across the room, wrinkled his brow and pinched his chin.

Lee hoped he had something helpful in mind.

"Considering that Jennifer is cleared," Peterson spoke slowly, "and that NSA and the FBI will go to bat for her I think all we really need to do is have her sign a nondisclosure agreement with National Aerospace." Peterson's words now came in a steady flow. "That would resolve the whole issue without anyone becoming too upset. Besides, there's nothing about this affair that National Aerospace would want to be in the press. If that cute face were plastered on the front page of every newspaper and on every TV screen in America accompanied by bad press for National Aerospace—well, I just can't see them letting that happen."

He agreed with everything Peterson said, except for one thing. Jennifer's face was in no way cute. It was absolutely, stunningly beautiful. But this wasn't the forum for such a discussion. He glanced at Jennifer. Her arms were no longer folded. She appeared more embarrassed than worried by this turn in the discussion.

Lee heard the door behind him opened.

A familiar voice came over his shoulder. "What in the world have you stirred up now?" Joe asked as he walked around to an empty chair.

It was a good thing they had a game plan for this.

When Joe turned to be seated Lee could see the smile on his face. That was good. But it also meant Barry was here. He prayed the NSA agent was, too.

As Barry entered the makeshift conference room a dark-suited stranger followed. The stranger was followed by Agent Bastian.

Thank you, Lord.

Even without NSA's help Lee already decided nobody would run roughshod over Jennifer. If they tried he had another bug-infested cave waiting for them.

"Brandt?" That wasn't a good sign. Barry never called him that. "You're in a lot of trouble. I want to know everything you and that student from the university found out. You compromised our security by bringing her in." Barry was always quick to speak and to throw his weight around.

Lee wasn't sure how much Joe knew about the security breach. But since Barry's attack was all threat and no substance Joe must not have revealed any details of this case to Barry. He would let Barry run for a while giving him some rope. If Barry started to come down on Jennifer he would yank the noose, hard.

"You disclosed proprietary company and classified military information to her all without proper authorization."

You shouldn't have said that, Barry.

Barry continued his rant. "You could lose your job—even spend a little time in prison along with your college—"

"Barry, that's enough!" His voice surprised him with its ferocity. "You will leave Jennifer out of this. Her participation was absolutely necessary to discover the terrorist and drug-cartel activity within National Aerospace. She connected the dots and located the hackers they were using to get inside our firewalls."

Barry's mouth had closed and his eyes bulged at the words "terrorist and drug cartel activity." Barry's mouth opened again. "But—"

"I don't like buts, Barry. And if you even mention prosecuting Jennifer, or damaging her career in any way, yours is in trouble. You will see page after page in the press detailing how National Aerospace let terrorists and drug lords infiltrate the computing system that you and our illustrious CEO outsourced to a foreign company, giving away American jobs in the process. Besides, Jennifer has a Top Secret SCI clearance. I don't even think you know what that is. And she routinely works with the FBI and NSA. In case you haven't noticed both of those organizations are represented in this room."

The man in the dark suit had seated himself, but now he stood and faced Barry. "I'm Agent Stewart, NSA and you would be wise to listen to Mr. Brandt's advice. We don't want what we know to become public knowledge until we have found and dealt with all of the conspirators. Maybe not even then. Besides, until Mr. Brandt and Ms. Akihara brief us on what they found, evidently something that very nearly got them killed, we don't know for sure what, or whom, we're up against."

Barry closed his mouth, sat down, and slumped in his chair.

A picture popped into Lee's mind of Barry seated at the table choking on his own foot. He hadn't seen Barry humiliated before and he couldn't help enjoying it. He managed not to laugh. But even Joe, who personally had a lot at stake here was grinning from ear to ear at Lee's outburst.

Jennifer laid her hand over his and squeezed firmly. Apparently, his spirited defense pleased her. This was a very, very good sign.

Maybe the ump would reverse the call on the previous pitch. Maybe the sun would shine in Mudville after all. Maybe—he looked at Jennifer's face. Maybes weren't good enough. There were things he needed to know...soon.

Stewart focused on Peterson. "I suggest someone get a nondisclosure agreement form from National Aerospace and modify it as needed. We'll have Jennifer sign it. That will take care of everything that's already transpired and it will cover anything we might need to get into today. What do you think, Joe?"

The man nodded slowly. "A properly worded nondisclosure agreement would make me a lot more comfortable. Let's do it."

"The sooner, the better." Peterson added. "We'll need someone in management to take care of it. There's no one better qualified here than Lee's supervisor. Besides, he would have to leave before the briefing anyway—not properly cleared and no real need to know."

Barry rose with a scowl on his face and strode to the door. "I'll take care of it." He closed the door a little more firmly than necessary. Joe continued his grin.

The forecast today, sunny in Mudville.

Lee stood. "Do we need anyone else in the room before I brief you?"

Peterson looked around the table. "Let's go with this crew. We can bring others in if they're needed. But...there is one matter we need to attend to first."

Peterson pulled out a USGS topographical map of the mountains where Jennifer and Lee spent much of the day. He spread it out on the shop bench. "Mark the cave—the one with the guns."

Lee smiled as he placed a small X on the map using his right hand, while his left hand, visible only to Jennifer, scratched his rear end. He heard a muffled giggle.

"Bastian, we need you to retrieve the automatic weapons the perpetrators left in the cave right here." Peterson pointed to the mark Lee made then handed the map to Bastian.

"Sure thing, boss."

"And Bastian?"

"Yes?"

"Get a hazmat suit to wear in the cave and don't come back without the weapons."

"Wouldn't think of it. See you in about an hour."

Only if you listen to your boss.

Bastian closed the door behind him.

"Will he wear a suit?" Lee asked, noting that Peterson hadn't told the man why he needed a protective suit.

"I told him to, but he doesn't always listen to me." Peterson shrugged.

When the door closed, Jennifer sat with her hand over her mouth. Her body shook with each partially stifled giggle.

Stewart looked at Joe and raised his upturned palms. Joe shrugged in return. For now he would let them remain clueless.

Lee clasped his hands and turned to look at Joe. "Before I begin. Joe, how is Randy? I saw them shooting at him, but Jennifer and I were on the run. We couldn't tell what happened at the gate shack."

Joe dipped his head and smiled. "Randy came through without a scratch, otherwise the response to you two being missing would have been much slower. Who knows? Randy may have saved your lives."

"That's good." He took a breath and let it out slowly. "I guess Jennifer and I owe Randy one. OK. Some military data were viewed by one of the Indian contractors. These data somehow slipped through the screening process when we loaded the development environment."

He remained purposely vague, being kind for Joe's sake. The data-security breach during data load was National Aerospace's fault which would reflect upon Joe. "Of course, the guy who accessed the data suddenly returned to Bangalore before we discovered the breach. As nearly as I can tell we were supposed to discover the violation, realize the perpetrator was gone, and since no real damage was done chalk one up for experience. They thought we would forget the incident while we promised our superiors this would never happen again. But this was only a diversion to give the imposter a way to disappear after he completed his real mission leaving us thinking the incident was closed."

Joe pounded his fist into his knee. "How in the world did we let an imposter get in?"

Peterson sighed loudly. "I won't even attempt to describe the hodgepodge India has to maintain identity. Many Indians can't prove they were even born, let alone who they are. It would be trivial to slip in someone with a false identity, especially a new hire."

Joe raised his eyebrows and stared at Lee. "So

what was the real mission?"

Lee glanced at Jennifer. When she returned his gaze, he smiled and nodded towards her. "Jennifer should take over from here. Everything we learned from this point forward was due to her genius."

Jennifer's initial look of surprise gave way to a smile when their gaze locked. He guessed Jennifer's stunning looks and her gender probably resulted in her being locked out of many good-old-boy meetings even when her work was being discussed. That wasn't going to happen today. He voluntarily gave up the floor to her for the sake of her career. When Lee sat down beside her she squeezed his hand.

Jennifer began to speak, laying out the entire conspiracy including the details of the analysis required and the facts she found. As she described running her analysis from the National Aerospace laptop, using her algorithm and NSA's Internet database, Agent Stewart winced a couple times. Jennifer would have a few wrinkles of her own to iron out.

She continued to explain her findings. "The imposter's objective was to get inside National Aerospace's firewalls. He left behind some very nasty, well-conceived Trojans. I've not seen anything quite like them in my experience. We found them on one laptop equipped with the company's VPN client. I analyzed them using some tools I developed for the FBI."

"So IPSec was how the Trojan got through our firewalls?" Joe asked.

"Only indirectly. In order for outgoing transmissions to get out through your firewall the Trojan applied a patch to your company's VPN client, which normally does use IPSec. The patch enabled it to send carefully crafted HTTP. So, to your proxy the transmission looked like a web browser going to some web site — nothing suspicious.

"However, I believe the HTTP contained encoded account and key information enabling the hacker who received it to login to your VPN server. As long as the hacker logged in within a few seconds the *borrowed* key would be good and he would be successful. Once logged in the hacker would appear to be a valid employee who was working off site. Masquerading as a legitimate company employee, the hacker could access all resources for which the employee was authorized — personal information, proprietary information, classified data — everything.

"Over time, Mr. Morrison, they could penetrate deeply into National Aerospace's data infrastructure and acquire a lot of data that could do a lot of damage to a lot of people."

"Not good." Joe groaned. "And where was the hacker, or hackers, located?"

Jennifer looked at Stewart. "Does anyone need to leave before I answer that, Mr. Stewart?"

Stewart glanced around the room and then shook his head. "No. But, Peterson, will you please sit by the door and make sure no one enters while Jennifer completes her briefing."

After Peterson scooted his chair in front of the door, Jennifer continued. "The hackers I detected were all at least four IP-address hops away. Each went through a series of compromised machines to disguise their locations. Their physical locations were Iran, Yemen, Colombia, and northern Mexico."

Joe whistled through his teeth. "I can see if you

upset their applecart you would be destroying months, or perhaps years, of preparation to get inside our company. We have a ton of information that a terrorist could use to cripple weapons systems or sell to raise money. There's classified military data, trade secrets, and other proprietary information, right down to identity information for our employees."

Jennifer continued. "It appears the bad guys wanted ongoing and expanded access inside of National Aerospace. They developed a second Trojan designed to infect the laptops employees frequently carry home. They wanted to infect a sufficient number of machines to intercept all types of data Mr. Morrison mentioned. A laptop at home could send data directly to machines anywhere in the world without having to deal with your web proxy or your VPN—much like when an employee uses split-tunnel access."

Joe hung his head and shook it. "That's one reason why we've recently eliminated split-tunnel access at National Aerospace."

Peterson sat motionless in his chair staring at Jennifer. "Do you have information linking the hackers to a specific organized-crime, or terrorist organization?"

Jennifer nodded. "Some information. We tied the IP addresses to routers recently used by two Islamic jihadist organizations and two Latin American drug cartels. I won't mention names here for security reasons...and because my findings need further analysis."

Stewart leaned forward in his chair. "Jennifer, we ran the trap line from evidence taken from the black SUV. In addition to fleas, we found other information we linked to a terrorist group operating in South

America, one which has ties to Al Qaeda. There were also ties to a drug cartel operating in northern Mexico. So this seems to confirm most of your preliminary findings."

Peterson turned towards Stewart. "It also confirms that these networks of terrorists are getting pretty close to home."

Joe ran his scowl around the room. "But National Aerospace is home. And that's alarming."

Stewart leaned forward in his chair and propped his forearms on his knees. "Well, gentlemen, it may very well be that Jennifer and Lee, while violating some protocols, have stopped a serious national security threat, as well as a serious industrial espionage threat to National Aerospace,"

Peterson stopped writing on his notepad. "Anything else?"

"No, Agent Peterson."

A strategy session ensued until 4:30 p.m., when Dan Robbins interrupted the group. "FYI, an injured man wandered into a clinic about eight miles from here," Dan reported. "He acted suspiciously. The doctor saw the bulletins released to the media so he called us. We arrested the guy. Funny thing—the man was all swollen up, had difficulty breathing, and had a pink rash over most of his body."

Lee became concerned about his suggestion to send Bastian to get the abandoned weapons. How should he phrase this concern? He needed to say something. "Petersen, what if Bastian has trouble on the mountain?"

"Don't worry, Lee. I'll take good care of Bastian. He has a radio and we have a chopper on alert in case we need it."

Jennifer grinned, while Joe Morrison gave another palms-up shrug.

Since Lee was ignorant of protocol and politics in the FBI he thought it best to leave Joe clueless on this matter. Peterson seemed like a good guy. He didn't want to create any trouble for the FBI agent. But if Bastian didn't follow his boss's orders he would pay a very unpleasant price.

Peterson raised his wrist and glanced at his watch. "It's 5 p.m. and I think we've accomplished just about everything we can at this time. Are we ready to let these two spelunkers go?"

Stewart stood. "Before we adjourn, there's one more item we need to cover. Jennifer and Lee, the media will swarm around you at every opportunity. Under no circumstances are you to discuss this incident with anyone unless directed to do so by myself, or Agent Peterson. When the media sees you're not answering their questions, they'll likely start throwing their hypotheses at you and asking you to confirm them. If they do simply tell them you cannot affirm or deny any statements presented to you by the media. Refer them to the FBI. Do you both understand?"

Lee nodded. "Got it."

"Sure, I understand." Jennifer answered.

Peterson stood. "Meeting adjourned."

When they left the makeshift conference room Jennifer pulled Lee to a stop. "So we're supposed to say we can't confirm a statement made by the press, even if we really can confirm it?"

"That's about the size of it."

Jennifer tapped Peterson on the shoulder, interrupting his conversation with Stewart. "Peterson, I know you're impounding my car for evidence, but I left a few things in it. Things I need. Is there any way I can get them tonight? Then there's also the issue of transportation for Lee and me."

"We can get your things, Jennifer," Peterson glanced at Stewart. Stewart nodded, and Peterson continued. "Why don't you and Lee ride over to Kerbyville in my car? We'll have the police get the items for you."

"May I ride along, too?" Stewart asked.

"Sure." Peterson replied. "Unless you want to spend the night in the Benson's shop."

After the short ride to the Kerbyville Police Station from the Benson's house, Stewart unbuckled his seat belt and swiveled to face Jennifer and Lee, who sat in the back seat. His pursed lips stretched into a smile. "Jennifer, NSA is very grateful for your services and has agreed to provide you with the use of a vehicle until you get yours back, or until you make other arrangements."

"Thanks. Thank you very much."

After Peterson parked in front of the police station he turned to Lee and Jennifer. "The motivation for the attack on you two is gone, but with these jihadist types, you never know what twisted logic drives them. To be safe I'm having both of your apartments watched tonight while your *friend* is running loose."

Stewart pointed across the street. "There's your vehicle, Jennifer."

When she glanced across the street, her eyes widened and her mouth dropped open.

20

Lee watched as Jennifer completed her external inspection of the car provided, a large, black SUV, eerily similar to the one that had chased them last night.

Twin frown lines remained frozen on her brow. She opened the door and slipped behind the wheel. After scanning the interior a smile replaced the frown. The ironic coincidence looked like it may not be disastrous after all.

Jennifer was clearly being wooed big time by NSA. The events of the past twenty-four hours undoubtedly played an important role in their determination not to let Jennifer slip away from them.

Lee shared both their sentiment and their determination.

Stewart walked across the street and handed Jennifer some keys and papers. He couldn't hear the words they exchanged, but Jennifer nodded and smiled. When Stewart walked away Jennifer motioned to him. "Come on. I'm driving you home."

That was an invitation he would not turn down. It would take at least an hour to drive back to the city. Finally, they could talk without wondering if they were uttering their last words. Lee hoped it would be an hour of leisurely driving with no more nerve-wracking suspense. However, with Jennifer at the wheel and her mind in gear, he wasn't sure what the hour might hold.

When the car rolled away from the curb, Lee followed suit with the conversation. "Jenn, there's a lot I'd like to know about you. I got a crash course in your character over the past twenty-four hours. But I—"

"Did you pass the course, or just crash?" Her face displayed a smirky smile.

"Uh, I don't know about me, but you more than passed my test."

The smirk faded. "So, how did you test me?"

"Let's see, there was the time in the cave, just before we climbed out, and then on the Benson's front lawn—"

"Come on. You know what I mean." Twin frown lines appeared between her dark eyebrows. "I seldom—well, actually, I never go out with guys. So I don't get any feedback. None that really matters."

He decided to jump in with both feet. "So you've never dated at all? That's hard to believe. I mean look at—"

"That's what I don't mean. Sure guys are always looking at me, or they're leering. Do you know how that makes me feel?"

"It's hard for me to imagine. Devalued as a person?"

"That's an understatement."

"I'm sorry you've experienced all that sordid, hurtful—not all guys are like that."

She stared into his eyes. She was supposed to be watching the road. Her look was searching, exploring, and it contained something else. Hoping?

"The jury's still out on your assertion about all guys."

"I can't believe you sent the jury into deliberation

before I could even present my closing arguments."

"Look, it's my life, my heart, and my courtroom. My rules too, so I can call the jury back anytime I choose. But first, you looked like you wanted to ask me something."

She read him well. A good thing if they were forming a permanent bond.

"I wanted to ask you about the guys you do associate with, classmates, coworkers..."

"The guys at school are all either somehow intimidated—"

"Gee, I can't imagine why."

She gave him her laser look. "See, even you think of me as, well, different. I really hate that."

"You are different and I love that." He came dangerously close to an admission that was still just a suspicion in his heart. He needed to tread carefully. Not overstate things.

Jennifer smiled and it looked as if she was blushing. "What am I going to do about you, Mr. Brandt?"

"I've got a suggestion, Miss Akihara." His remark drew a mischievous smile. Good. "But first, you were going to tell me about your friends at school."

"The only guys I would label as friends are computer geeks. We get along because of shared interests. They're protective. They watch out for me, but that's as close a relationship as I have with anybody, male or female."

"No girlfriends?" He was puzzled.

"None since I was twelve or thirteen. Girls can be really cruel if you don't conform to their codes of conduct, dress, and certain other things completely outside of one's control."

Sure glad I'm a guy.

He glanced at her face. He could see a whole host of "certain other things." "That's too bad. I can introduce you to some women about your age who would be real friends."

"If you're suggesting women at your church I've already experienced cruel, churchgoing women."

"A church is like a wheat field. You'll find both wheat and weeds there. Sounds like you found some weeds. But there's genuine wheat growing there if you look for it without letting the weeds discourage you. But may I sum up what you've told me? I want to be sure I understand."

Jennifer looked into his face like a serious reader turning the page in a suspense novel. "OK. Tell me what you heard."

He took a deep breath and exhaled. "Let's see, you haven't gone on any dates. How am I doing so far?"

"Absolutely correct. The harassment from guys began before I was old enough to date. If you don't count going out for pizza with five or six computer nerds, then I've never dated."

This was unbelievable, but Jennifer despised lying. Though difficult to believe it was his good fortune. "And you've had no close girlfriends—"

"That's true. But tell me something. How do you know you can believe me?"

"Now we're getting into an area I'm familiar with." He placed his hand on her shoulder. "I would trust you with my life. In fact, I already have several times."

"But those were times when I was in danger, too. It could have been, you know, self preservation—purely self interest."

He looked at her until she returned his gaze. "But not when you were falling off the rock. You kept silent to save my life."

Jennifer had no reply.

Lee tried to see what was in her eyes, but she looked straight ahead, far down the road. From the side, her large brown eyes appeared to be brimming with tears. At least the right eye was. That wasn't like the Jennifer he knew. But maybe it was like the Jennifer he was beginning to know.

Should I or shouldn't I? Stupid question.

"I'm thirty years old. I've been looking for someone for several years—someone to spend a lifetime with. I think someone like you. But everyone I've met has fallen short of—"

"How do you know I wouldn't fall short like the others?"

He paused as he sought an appropriate way to express what was on his heart. "I'm just like most people, a person looking for genuine love. But love isn't just feelings. That's where so many people go wrong. Real love is a choice, a commitment to never ever abandon a person for as long as you live. You choose to love them for a lifetime. I've seen what commitment means to you especially when the chips are down. I don't think anything could pry you loose from a commitment you made. That's how I know you aren't like the others."

She didn't reply. She brushed her eyes and stared far down the road.

Seconds went by. They seemed like hours.

"Lee"—she took a deep breath and exhaled— "what if you committed to something or someone?"

Was it too soon for them to be having this

conversation? He looked at her again. Stupid question. "I hope my commitment would be just like yours."

A smile spread across her face. She brushed more tears away. "That's good to know."

His spirits began to soar. This conversation far exceeded his expectations, but so had Jennifer. "There's a whole lot more I want to know about you—things that just don't come up when goons are shining a flashlight at you on a cave wall so they can blow you away."

"That does sort of restrict the scope of the conversation." She sighed. "So ...what do you want to know? Ask away."

No woman had ever given him that invitation. But then, he'd never met anyone like Jennifer. "OK. What's your favorite song?"

"I thought you might ask me what my favorite hymn was."

"I didn't honestly think you had one."

"Well I do...sort of...not exactly a hymn. I heard a song on the radio while I was scanning for some good music. An older song. The DJ said it was from the '90s. But the words pulled me right in. I heard a real joy in the music, the rhythm, and the words. I immediately loved it. Later I searched the net, found the CD, and bought it. Then I discovered all of the other songs were openly Christian. That's when I realized the love the artist sang about was really between him and God, not love between a man and a woman. That kind of relationship with God, if He were real, became something I wanted for myself. But I didn't know how to get it, or if it was even possible."

So much for hard-core agnosticism. Jennifer was a seeker.

"Wow. It sounds as good as any hymn I know. What was the song? Maybe I know it."

She hesitated before answering. "It's called 'Living in the Light of Your Love,' by Al Denson."

He smiled at her answer and the open door it gave him. "I have that CD in my collection, too. Great song and a great artist." He paused. "What do you think about the part of the title that says 'the light of your love'?"

She gave him a corner-of-the-eye glance. "You heard me in the cave, didn't you?"

"Yeah."

"Well, when the song got to where two hearts became one and I realized the songwriter was talking about a really intimate relationship, it attracted me and frightened me at the same time, because the relationship would be between me and God, not between just a man and woman."

How should I say this? Help me, Lord.

"When the relationship is based upon the right things, the relationship between a man and his wife and the relationship between a person and God have a lot in common."

His comment drew her laser look. "Come on, Lee, I'm not a churchgoer, but I'm not naïve, either. I think you're a smooth talker who—"

"No, Jenn. That's the way it's supposed to be. Both relationships are intimate. Both are based upon love. Not the Hollywood fantasy version of love, but an unselfish love that always considers the other person first. Both are meant to be a lasting commitment. The love doesn't dissolve as soon as either party decides they want to walk away. If you want to read about this kind of love, read First Corinthians chapter thirteen in your Bible. It explains it better than I ever could."

There were far too many coincidences for what was happening in their lives to be accidental. He wanted to probe deeper. "One more question about the song—when did you get the CD?"

"About a week ago."

God's timing was impeccable. "Jenn, does that tell you anything?"

She sat silent and stared down the road for a few moments. "Maybe...something like—"

"Like maybe He's inviting you to be living in the light of His love?"

He was certain God had been at work in Jennifer's life, drawing her to Himself, before he even met her. "You and I called on Him several times in the last two days. Did He answer?"

It was silent in the SUV for several seconds. Jennifer gave a slight nod and spoke softly. "Yes...maybe not exactly how I thought He would answer, but He always answered."

"Sometimes it's incredible how God answers. I think I know what's best, and then He answers in some entirely unexpected way making it so much better—better like—"

His words were stolen from him by a glance at Jennifer. They had rounded a turn causing the late afternoon sun to light her face. Struck again by Jennifer's beauty, his mind and emotions began racing out of control.

He needed to slow things down for Jennifer's sake, as well as his own. "I didn't mean to get into a heavy discussion."

She reached across and squeezed his hand. "It's OK. I didn't mind."

She wasn't making it easy to slow anything down. Maybe a change of subject would help. "I never did find out the answer to my original question. What's your favorite song?"

She released his hand and put hers back on the steering wheel. "It's a really old one. Artists still record it, but only one person knows how to sing it. The person who wrote it."

"The name of the song is?"

She reached for his hand again. "It's 'You've Got a Friend,' but only when Carole King sings it."

"Surely you lie."

Her hand went back to the steering wheel. "You know better than that, Mr. Brandt."

"Bad choice of words. You surprised me. It's at the top of my list, too. But I also like the way she sings "Way Over Yonder.""

Jennifer laughed softly. "Well, I guess we're musically compatible. I have that CD, too."

"It's more than just the music." He'd done it again. But what he said was the truth.

Jennifer grew quiet and pensive for the next few minutes.

He had probed deeply and possibly had jumped the gun with some of his assertions. He stopped asking questions.

But they had shared life and almost certain death with each other. After those experiences how could the deep issues of life be off limits? And Jennifer had answered even the serious questions. She was honest almost to a fault if such a thing was possible.

During the intermission he slipped into a silent conversation.

I've waited for a long time, now. I've seen no one I

could picture spending my life with. I know Jennifer is still a seeker, not yet a believer. This isn't what I expected, Lord. I really need to know what's happening here.

He was willing to wait on God, as well as Jennifer's response to Him. He glanced her way. He couldn't wait much longer. If she wasn't God's choice for him, having to give Jennifer up after twenty-three hours and twelve minutes of knowing her would be, by far, the hardest thing he had ever done.

After a few minutes Jennifer gave him several quick glances. She took her right hand off the wheel of the big SUV and held his left hand.

"Now it's my turn to ask you some questions. OK?"

What she asked was only fair.

"OK. Fire away."

"Are you sure, Lee?"

"I think so. Why?"

"Because some guys have started squirming and weaseling out when I ask them questions. You're not going to weasel out on me, are you?"

"No, Jenn. No weaseling out."

She looked at him without smiling. Her eyes were intense, but they displayed something less than her laser look. "So you'll do your best to answer every question truthfully?"

What did she want him to do? Place his hand on a Bible and swear to tell the truth? "I'll answer as best I can."

"OK. We've grown very close during the past twenty-four hours." She opened his hand and interlaced their fingers. "That's pretty obvious. Suppose my character and personality were unchanged, but I was obese or ugly. Would we be sitting here holding hands? Would we be this close?"

The first question and already the thumbscrews were painfully tight. This woman was good at that. He couldn't blame her for asking the question. But he needed to tell the truth or he could kiss her goodbye.

No...there wouldn't even be a goodbye kiss.

Based on what she had told him Jennifer wasn't even looking for a man. They were only a source of trouble and pain for her. There was so much riding on his answer.

"Lee, you disappeared on me. Where did you go? To weasel land? Tell me, would we still be this close?"

He needed to answer her and only the truth would keep him in the hunt. "No, Jenn. We wouldn't."

Jennifer's face fell. She slumped behind the wheel, hardly looking up enough to see the road ahead. Had he really sucked all the life out of her with his answer? She didn't look like the same person.

"Please let me explain."

"Go ahead." Her monotone said she was hardly interested.

He squeezed her limp hand. "When did we really draw close?"

"I thought we did in the cave, but I'm not so sure now."

"Remember how dark it was where we spent most of that time?" He didn't wait for a reply. "There was no way I couldn't see what you really looked like and—"

"No more baloney, Lee. You knew! From the second I walked into Howie's office, you knew."

"I know, but let me get to my real point. If you were by most people's standards, unattractive, it wouldn't have made any difference to me. Your character and your personality drew me to you. I can easily see myself spending the rest of my life with that person, no matter whether they were ugly, plain, or just plain beautiful."

Jennifer sat in silence. She was ruminating on his answer. "And what about the obese part?"

"It's irrelevant. In that case, we wouldn't be here having this discussion. You would have gotten stuck under the big overhang and the goons would have shot you."

"Lee, I said no more baloney. Answer the question. You're not going to weasel out of it by stupid, twisted logic."

Why had he said that? It was true but—"I get it. The obesity issue has not been sufficiently dealt with."

She glared at him. Her hand wasn't limp. It was crushing his. "Not even close."

"Jenn, I need to know. Are we talking morbidly obese here?"

Jennifer's voice had the edge of a razor blade. "Yes. I'm morbidly obese."

Lord, help me here.

The revelation came from somewhere deep inside. God had already answered this question in His word. He took a deep breath and plunged into his answer. "People are sometimes sturdily built because of genetics—maybe even a little plump. But unless they have some untreated medical problem, morbid obesity is something they do to themselves. The Bible calls that thing gluttony, eating too much because you like eating. God says it's a sin, a character weakness. I wouldn't want to spend my life with someone who hadn't dealt with that issue. An issue that's actually between them and God."

Jennifer didn't reply immediately. She sat silently,

staring down the road with a squinting frown on her face. "OK, what if I was in the process of dealing with the issue, but was still, you know, too heavy?"

If this was her litmus test she was milking it for all it's worth.

"Then I'd be glad to stick with you and help you deal with it. In the meantime, I wouldn't be looking for anyone else."

There was no comeback from Jennifer. She sat still and silent for a full minute. Then she lifted her head, looked far down the road and took a deep breath like an underwater swimmer coming up for air. She smiled and squeezed his hand. There were no more questions.

She smiled at me. Does that mean I passed the test? Maybe I aced it.

He would have to wait for Jennifer to let him know in her own time and in her own way.

21

Jennifer drove the big car slowly as she navigated the streets near Lee's apartment.

"You probably should drop me off at a car rental place. There's one about ten blocks from here. They stay open late and I'm going to need a car."

"Since I'm picking you up for church in the morning. Can't you wait until tomorrow to get a car? What you really need is a good night's sleep."

"What if something comes up tonight, Jenn, and I can't get to you?"

"Nothing's going to happen tonight. Our apartments are being watched. Are you a worrier? Because if you are I need to know now, so I can learn to deal with it."

"I just have, well, concerns. At least until this is all wrapped up in a nice little bow."

"OK, let's get you a car. But I think you should go for a small, white, 2001 sedan from Rent-A-Wreck."

"No, thank you."

She gave him a melodramatic, wide-eyed stare. "Lee Brandt, are you insulting my taste in cars?"

"No. It would just bring back too many memories."

She reached for his hand. "They weren't all bad memories, were they?"

"Yes, Jenn. In your car, they were *all* bad memories."

Hide and Seek

She was quiet for a moment. "I guess those were all bad—while we were in the car that is." She squeezed his hand. "But the cave—"

"That's the rental lot on the right." He really wanted to hear Jennifer's take on the cave, but they were both fading fast. "Have you got anything to write on?"

"I don't have a clue. I just hopped in and started driving this thing. Look in the glove box."

"Hmmm. A gum wrapper and a small, sticky-note tablet. It'll do." He pulled his space pen from his pocket. "Here's my phone number. If anything comes up, or if you get the willies, call me and I'll be right over."

"You'll be right over where, Lee?"

"I must be getting pretty wiped out. Didn't even remember that I don't have your address or phone number."

Jennifer looked at him and shook her head. "You're a smooth operator, Lee Brandt." She took a sticky note from him and snatched his pen. "Just remember this. No guy has ever gotten what you are about to get."

He hoped no other guy ever would.

Jennifer wrote down her address and phone number. She gave him his pen and he gave her a droopy smile.

Running on empty both mentally and physically, he got out and walked to the driver's side.

Jennifer's window slid down. "Here's something to tide you over until morning." She grabbed his chin with one hand and the back of his head with the other, twisted his head ninety degrees and planted a kiss on his cheek. "It's been a wonderful date, Lee, but I broke

197

curfew by twenty hours. I might have to ground myself."

"I've never had a date quite like that one either, Jenn. But then I haven't dated since I was seventeen, so I have no real basis for comparison."

"No other dates? Then I hold the number one rating on your date list. But what happened when you were seventeen?"

"I made a decision not to date. I'll tell you about it sometime."

Jennifer's frown and cocked head said she had questions, but she didn't ask them. When the time was right, he would explain.

"See you at 8:45 a.m. I think we're both going to need a big coffee before church in the morning."

He dipped his head. "A triple-shot mocha at least. The pastor frowns on people falling asleep during his sermons."

"Gotta run, Lee. It may take an hour to work this big beast into my tiny parking space."

"Goodnight, Jenn." There was a lot more he wanted to say before the goodnight part. But it would have to wait until tomorrow. Tomorrow.

He was delighted that she seemed willing, even eager, to attend church with him. It was quite an ending to a day with such a terror-filled beginning.

Lee scanned the rental lot. One light-colored sedan of the same make. Unlike Jennifer's, it was brand new. He took it. The price was right. If his insurance agent came through the price wouldn't matter.

Through blurred vision he managed to sign the papers. He drove into his driveway as darkness fell, walked to his bedroom, set the alarm for 7:45 a.m., pulled off his shoes, and crashed.

****

Lee pulled the pillow over his exposed ear. "Not the alarm already. I just laid down."

Eventually, he relented and rolled over to shut off the CD his alarm was playing. He looked out the window. The sun had topped the Cascades on a beautiful, sunny, Sunday morning. But best of all, a beautiful woman was going to pick him up in an hour. He needed to shower and dress, but the previous thirty-six hours had emptied his energy reserves.

Lee stumbled through the routine of getting ready for church. At 8:30 he studied himself in his bedroom mirror. He looked presentable. Well, everything except the foot-long, gauze-covered abrasion on his right forearm looked presentable. His red badge of courage. He was running for his life. *It fits.*

At 8:44 a.m. her car rolled along the street in front of his apartment. This was his second appointment with Jennifer and she was right on time, again. Prompt. It pleased him. But despite her temper and an IQ significantly higher than his, there wasn't a single thing about Jennifer he didn't like. On the flip side, there was a whole lot to like.

He grabbed his Bible and hurried out the door. He could barely see Jennifer through the dark glass, but his first view of her reminded him of last night's omission. He meant to tell her how people dressed at his church.

Maplewood Community was a come-as-you-are congregation, but Lee wanted Jennifer to be as comfortable as possible during her first visit to his church. Maybe she was an as-you-are person and would be comfortable regardless.

He opened the passenger-side door and peered in.

She had dressed on the nice end of casual.

Perfect.

"Morning, Lee. How did you sleep?"

He looked at her long, dark hair, her brown, almond-shaped eyes and concluded she was totally and absolutely—

"Lee, where did you go? Are you awake, yet?"

"Uh...I think so."

She eyed him with suspicion. "I'm not convinced."

"I did have a little trouble waking up. Zonked for nearly eleven hours, but I'm still going to need coffee to get me through the morning." He slipped in and closed the door.

Jennifer pulled away from the curb. "Me, too. The exhaustion came from more than missing a night of sleep. We went through a lot of emotional stress. Things went up and down so fast, from we're alive to we're about to die—I got really wrung out." She paused and pointed towards his rental car. "Is that your parking spot?"

"That's my spot." He smiled and waited for her reaction.

"Don't tell me you actually rented a white car like mine."

"Not white, but close." He gave her a smug smile. "Ten years newer than yours, though."

She gave him a frowning glance. "Wait a minute. Mine had a lot of character."

"Unlike the characters who shot it." He had accidentally taken their conversation in an unintended direction. Maybe he could steer it back towards them.

Her twin frown lines appeared. "I wonder when

we'll get an update on the search for goon number three?"

He didn't want to see frowns on her face this morning. The day was too beautiful and Jennifer...well, she outshone even the day. One look at her and his mind was already—

"Lee? There's a question on the table."

Caught again.

He yawned much wider than his fatigue prompted him to do. "Uh, soon, hopefully. At least by tomorrow, when we see Peterson."

"I've been thinking about...you know, what they should do after they catch and convict him." She was smiling now.

He returned her smile. "I'm open to any punishment you can think of. As long as it's not illegal."

"How about sentencing him to ninety-nine years in the flea cave?"

"Hmmm. Each year he would have eleven months to think about the next March." He paused. "But can't we talk about something other than caves?"

She gave him a lingering glance. No smile. No frown. Her eyes were deep, brown pools. "Lee, caves aren't all bad. I...I fell in love with you in a cave."

That silenced him.

Jennifer took the conversation so far so fast he was left grasping for an appropriate reply.

"Just like Tom and Becky." He finally managed. *Why did I say that?* He hadn't a clue.

She was frowning again. "I'm not following you. Is that from some movie?"

"Didn't you read *Tom Sawyer* by Mark Twain? Probably when you were about ten or eleven?"

"No. I never read Mark Twain. Well, not exactly. We had to read *Huckleberry Finn* in junior high. I wasn't into Mark Twain at that age, so I checked out the book for reference and then just read the Cliffs Notes."

"So honest Jenn was sometimes deceptive?"

"I never said I was perfect." She grinned. "But tell me about Becky."Jennifer pulled into the coffee shop drive through. "But first you'd better tell me what you're having."

"A grande, triple-shot mocha." He dipped his head and smiled.

"Got it." A pleasant, upbeat-sounding voice came from the speaker.

Jennifer thought for a second. "Make it two of those, please."

The speaker squawked again. "I'll have your total at the window."

Jennifer turned to him, waiting for his synopsis of *Tom Sawyer*.

"Becky Thatcher. Tom is head over heels for her. She's his first girlfriend. Tom thinks she's beautiful and, like a fool, he's always trying to impress her."

"It fits so far." Jennifer grinned. "Keep going."

"They get lost in a cave and Injun Joe turns up there. He wants to permanently silence Tom."

"Sounds familiar."

They rolled up to the window. He handed Jennifer his coffee-shop credit card. She looked at it for a moment. "You must be a heavy drinker."

"At times. You drove me to it."

"You actually came up with that before we got the caffeine. You amaze me sometimes, Lee Brandt."

The morning sun lit up her smiling face.

Not half as much as you amaze me, Jennifer Akihara.

His glance at her derailed his train of thought. "Let's see...uh...Joe chases Tom and Becky through the cave with a big knife."

"I can identify with that." Jennifer braked to a stop at the sign.

He pointed. "Turn left here and the church is about one mile ahead. Back to the story. Tom saves Becky. There's a kiss somewhere in there. Can't remember just—"

"I hope Tom appreciated it." Jennifer glanced at him.

She was smiling. Her smile, with the sunlight shining through the window on her hair, once again created a train wreck in his mind, destroying his comeback for Jennifer's comment.

"Let's see, when they get out of the cave, Tom's a hero."

"That's where the analogy breaks down, Lee. You went from potential hero to pure goat, but only for a little while." Jennifer smiled again, causing a third train wreck in his mind.

She glanced at his face and prompted him. "What happens next?"

Some women would have gloated over their power to attract and distract men.

The story. Get back to it, man. You're not done, yet.

"Uh. Oh, yes. After the initial popularity, Becky goes back to her upper-crust social class, leaving Tom dejected."

"Bummer." She shot him another glance. "By the way, I'm not the Becky type."

"I gathered that and I'm glad you aren't. But, Jenn, if you weren't reading Mark Twain when you were ten or eleven, what were you reading?"

"You don't want to know." Jennifer sounded a bit guarded.

He grew more curious. "Try me."

"If you insist." They were stopped at a red light. She stared at him for a moment. "Introduction to Automata Theory, Languages and Computation—oh, and Compilers...the Dragon Book."

"Sorry I asked. I didn't even look at those until my master's program."

"I told you, Lee."

He sensed that somehow his left brain, murdered in the cave, had been resurrected. Now both sides ganged up on him.

Just do it, man!

"Jenn?"

"Yes?"

He put his left hand over Jennifer's right. She shoved her coffee cup into the cup holder and grabbed the wheel with her left hand. Her right hand clasped his.

"Jennifer Akihara, I love you, too."

"It took you long enough to say it. I'll assume you needed the caffeine."

"No. After yesterday, I just assumed you like suspense."

"Don't you lie to me, Lee Brandt. What you just told me, you knew yesterday and so did I."

He dipped his head. "You're right. I guess I've known since—"

"Since the close call with the flying-dirt machine gun."

Sometimes this woman knew him better than he knew himself. That was another reason to be scrupulously honest with her.

It was all on the table now. Both had shown their hands and neither of them sounded disappointed at the outcome. Maybe both had won.

He sure hoped so. And hope ran strong, because she was in good hands.

He didn't want to, as Jennifer said, be presumptuous with God, but...

Lord, I know she's a seeker. Don't You think it's time for her to become a finder?

Jennifer was, in his books, a keeper. Could he handle being a loser?

22

When Jennifer turned in at Maplewood Community Church, she noticed Lee was unusually antsy.

While they rolled through the parking lot his right heel tapped out a snappy rhythm on the floorboard. "Just so you know, nothing weird goes on at the church. No rattlesnake handling. The people are really nice. You're going to feel right at home."

"I'm sure I will."

Good grief, he's more nervous than I am. Oh yes, he's the worrier—or what was it—the man with concerns? At least they're thoughtful concerns. I can handle that.

She centered the car on her target parking space, pulled in and cut the engine.

Lee tried to open her door, but she stopped him. "C'mon, Lee. I'm geek girl. You don't have to do that to impress me."

"At least give me your arm so I can escort you."

"I guess geek girl can handle that." She restrained her response to a smile, but she nearly burst out laughing watching the confident, reliable man—the man who saved her life during several, danger-filled moments—become so frantic over making her feel comfortable.

When they approached the front of the building an usher at the sanctuary door turned to greet them. From his expression she concluded he was one of Lee's friends.

"Well hello, Lee and hey, it's the two celebrities."

"Jim, this is Jennifer. I found her in a cave out by Iron Mountain. Jennifer this is Jim Williamson, a personal friend. A guy who holds me accountable for my behavior."

"Accountable? Lee, are you sure you really want to account for all the things you do?" She didn't give him a chance to respond. "Well, Jim, I should tell you this caveman clubbed me and dragged me here to church this morning."

Jim gave her a warm smile. "I'm sorry, Jennifer. We take them any way we can get them. Welcome to Maplewood Community Church."

Jennifer noticed Lee's friend tap him on the shoulder. After they passed Jim, she caught a glimpse of him standing in the doorway with two thumbs-up. That was good. Someone close to Lee, someone he trusted, approved of her.

It seemed to Jennifer as though every eye in the building were on Lee and her as they made their way to a seat midway down the aisle. There were more brief introductions to people who seemed sincerely friendly—people who weren't pretentious—people Jennifer felt drawn to though she had just met them.

When the worship leader took his place to start the service Lee whispered to her, "This guy likes the old hymns. That's probably all we'll get today."

"Maybe I'll like them, too. By the way, I notice we're back to whispering again."

"Only for the next hour."

The first hymn started. As the lyrics displayed on the overhead screen Lee sang them.

She studied the words to this old hymn.

He hideth my soul in the cleft of the rock.

The hymn reminded her of their experience on the chimney wall. The context of the cleft in the song was different. God led her to the cleft on the cave wall that saved her life. In the song God hid a person's immortal soul in a protected place, and then covered it with his hand. A soul protected forever.

God saved her mortal body and Lee's, too, by hiding them in the cleft. But how much more secure to know one's immortal soul was covered by the hand of God for eternity.

Eternity. An indescribable concept the mathematical symbol, the lemniscate, couldn't really convey. A symbol for the incomprehensible. Was the infinite, eternal God also incomprehensible?

Mathematics seemed so precise to her. Mathematical propositions were so provably true and correct she hadn't really thought how imprecise mathematics became on the fringes. The precision was lost until somewhere along the edges nothing was enumerable or computable. There, only an Infinite Being could possibly make sense of things. He would have to reveal the infinite things to finite human beings in a way that made sense to them. If He didn't they would never understand.

Why had she never thought about this before? So that's how God became comprehensible to people.

He reveals Himself. Is that what He's been doing with me?

The mysteries she probed with her algorithms all the way to the mathematical edges—where Turing machines never halt—where formal grammars lack the ability to specify—where recursive functions perform another recursion and that without end—beyond all that was computable, comprehensible, and enumerable, God was barely beginning. He extended infinitely beyond the edges to—

Jennifer shivered as an overpowering sense of awe overtook her. Beyond all she explored there was God. One could only reach Him by God reaching out. She knew without a doubt He was reaching out to her and she wanted to respond.

The first song ended and another began. Still thinking about the message of the first song Jennifer remained humbled and awestricken that a few simple words from a song, capturing only a tiny fraction of God's revelation to human beings, could so surpass any knowledge she could acquire on her own.

She prided herself on being someone who could do everything by herself and relying only on herself. The last thirty-six hours proved her self-reliance to be mostly self-deception.

She needed Lee in the cave and he needed her. But they both needed God to make it through. Maybe that's how life was supposed to be, consisting of vital relationships between people, and between individuals and God. That would be far better than trying to make it through alone.

The song service ended and the pastor walked to the podium.

"It's only two weeks until Resurrection Sunday. We'll probably get some kind of message about that," Lee leaned close and whispered.

The pastor was a soft-spoken man, but he spoke firmly and with great conviction. His subject was a set of claims Jesus made about Himself. Jesus said He was the Way, the Truth, the Life, and also the Resurrection.

Pastor Nelson clearly explained each concept he

introduced. "The Way" was an exclusive claim.

Jennifer had no problem with that concept, because truth was, by definition, exclusive. Like a correct mathematical answer, all other answers were wrong.

As for the Truth, the pastor's explanation surprised her. It seemed strange that truth wasn't embodied in a mathematical equation or a philosophical argument.

"I am the Truth," Jesus stated. Truth was a living person.

Jennifer could see clearly if someone relied on the wrong source for truth they would miss everything that mattered. If she missed Jesus she would miss the very thing she held in the highest regard, the truth. When she said in the cave she could see the light and it was wonderful, she knew Whom she needed, but she didn't understand His nature, or how to reach Him.

Prayer, yes, they prayed and God heard them.

But "The Way" was Jesus. He was the missing ingredient she needed in order to reach God. But knowing this still left her wondering how she could bring Jesus into her life.

The words Pastor Nelson spoke next made her gasp. It was far simpler to accept Jesus than she imagined. A person needed to place their trust in Him and recognize Him for who He was—rather, who He should be for Jennifer, her Savior, and the Lord of her life.

She felt as if Pastor Nelson was speaking directly to her.

"If you believe God is prompting you to accept the Way He has prepared for you, that is, Jesus, I am asking that you answer His prompting by walking down here and meeting me. I will have someone meet with you and answer any questions you may have so you can leave here today knowing you have eternal life through a relationship with God made possible by Jesus Christ."

An African-American lady with a deep, rich, contralto voice began singing. The song, like the pastor's message, pulled gently, but persistently on her heart and mind.

Should she resist? She had neither the means nor any reason to do so. She hooked Lee's arm and pulled him close.

"I'm going up there now." She pointed to the front.

"You sure?"

"Positive."

"When we climbed out of the cave what did you mean about seeing the light?"

"I meant I was ready to do what I'm about to do."

He smiled. "Then go. Do you want me to come too?"

"This is a personal decision so I think I should go alone." She paused.

But afterward, she would never have to live life alone again. "But…I think I want to talk to a lady when I go up there."

"It's our policy. A lady always talks to a lady. Looks like you'll be talking with Mrs. Raugust. You'll like her. So go."

****

As Lee watched her walk to the front of the auditorium he recalled her revelation yesterday that

God was already working in her heart. He remembered her revelation this morning that she loved him.

What was unfolding in their lives was incredible.

He sought words to describe what God was orchestrating. When the words came, they brought a smile to his face.

Jenn, I do believe God set you up...just like Howie set us up.

23

Lee realized he was observing something in Jennifer's character he'd seen several times this weekend. If she thought something was right, she did it without hesitation, unreservedly, and unabashedly. There was no holding back with her. Except maybe to forgive someone who was being dishonest with her.

He smiled and vowed, for the second time, to be scrupulously honest with her. There would be no running through the flea cave for him.

Jennifer and Pastor Nelson exchanged a few words. The pastor introduced Jennifer to Mrs. Raugust and then the two women entered the counseling room at the left front corner of the sanctuary.

"Seal the deal," he whispered softly.

He remembered how close he came to turning down Howie's offer of his best and brightest computer-security specialist. What if he had refused the offer? The results would have been—they were unthinkable.

He needed to express his gratitude to the One who orchestrated the life-changing events leading up to this moment.

Thanks, for nudging me in the right direction. Several lives have been changed, including my own. I thank You also that many people's lives have been spared because of Jennifer's work. But I thank You most of all for the life that is right now being changed forever.

****

Lee opened the counseling-room door and stepped in. "Mrs. Raugust said you wanted to kill me, or something like that."

"I was just complaining because no one, including you, told me how simple it was to hook up with God."

"Your words tend to get pretty violent when you complain, Jenn."

A voice, vaguely familiar to Lee, came from somewhere near the choir-robe closet. "Violent words, perhaps. But not as violent as the next few moments will be."

Lee turned towards the voice. "Ram." Instantly he felt like they were back in Jennifer's car, being pursued on the freeway. "I thought you went home to Bangalore." He pulled Jennifer close with his left arm, and his gaze swept the room looking for a way of escape. He focused on the handle of a gun protruding from the holster under Ram's left arm. He did not want to volunteer any information or say anything to provoke the armed man. "What are you doing here?"

"I told you. I'm going to fill your next few moments with violence." Ram placed his hand on the handle of the gun. "Did you really think you could escape so easily? And my name is Abdul Matin Kassem. Apparently, you think you have made a new convert to your polytheistic religion. Father, Son, Holy Spirit—three gods. There is only one God. Allahu Akbar! You have done much harm to the cause of Allah, so you both will suffer much. Especially you, Lee."

Lee's fear transformed to anger. He clamped his mouth shut, so the words in his mind could not exit.

He must not say anything inflammatory.

Abdul's hand still hadn't pulled out the holstered weapon.

I've gotta keep him talking.

Abdul glared at him. "Move around the corner to the back. Do it, now!"

They began to move and as the distance between them shrank, Abdul pulled the Glock out of the holster.

"To the back." He replayed those words in his mind.

Abdul's plan was clear. He would kill them while he was at the back door of the building so he could escape through the alley behind the church.

There wasn't much time left. Whatever he chose to do must be done before Abdul stepped in front of the door.

Please provide a way for us. At least provide a way for me to protect Jenn and—

"Your suffering will come from watching the new convert, Jennifer, die first. As you are about to see hollow-point bullets can quickly reveal the ugliness behind false beauty."

No. God wouldn't allow that. Neither would he.

When the three stopped moving Abdul stood in front of the back door.

Lee felt Jennifer's body tense. Not the tensing of fear, but the tensing that comes before action. Thoughts flew through his mind, but he couldn't latch on to any of them. He was on the verge of panic when a moment of clarity came.

Jennifer wasn't afraid to die. She was going to sacrifice herself. He couldn't let that happen.

He wouldn't let Jennifer take a bullet. Not while there was still life in his body.

The barrel of the gun swung slightly off target when Abdul reached behind him to feel for the door handle.

He sensed this was his chance. A soft gasp came from Jennifer when she felt his muscles flex.

She knew and would try to make her move first.

Lee's gaze was still glued to Abdul.

Will he look back there again?

Abdul took one quick glance to be certain of his position in front of the door. Once again the gun swung slightly off to Lee's right away from Jennifer.

Jennifer launched her body at Abdul Matin Kassem.

In the same instant, Lee's coiled leg muscles propelled his body forward powered by fury and desperation. He was stronger. He crashed into Abdul first. The sweeping motion of his left hand pushed the Glock upward and off target. A single shot cracked loudly in the enclosed area.

Lee braced for the impact. When they hit the door he planned to disable Abdul or find a way to get his own hand on the gun.

Their impact with the door never came. Lee and Abdul flew through an open doorway into the alley. They sprawled onto the pavement.

Lee landed on top. He shoved his right hand under the man's chin. He found a choke-hold on his throat. Anger, fear, and the concomitant adrenaline energized his untrained hands as they squeezed Abdul's larynx. He was crushing it when two uniformed officers ripped him away.

They subdued Abdul while a third man pushed Lee away from the fray.

A fourth officer grabbed the Glock as it slid across

the pavement.

With his chest heaving Lee backed away from Abdul. Out of the corner of his eye he spotted Peterson running towards them. He exhaled deeply, releasing much more than just the air in his lungs. Maybe it was all finally over.

"Lee, I'm going to kill you!"

Not everything was under control.

A fifth SWAT team member pinned Jennifer's arms to her body. She now lay face down on the pavement a few feet behind where he and Abdul fell onto it.

Fear gripped him again. "It's OK! It's OK! She doesn't mean it literally!" He lowered his voice. "She never means it literally."

"Don't bet on it!" Jennifer shouted.

A uniformed officer lifted her to her feet, but still kept her arms clamped tightly to her sides.

Peterson stepped in trying to restore order to the scene—order which hadn't come even though the perpetrator was cuffed and laying on his face in the alley. "Let her go, Officer Ruska," Peterson's deep voice boomed. "It's OK. I know this young lady and, well…" Peterson's voice softened. "It's just OK."

When the policeman released her Lee took a step towards Jennifer, but she ran at him full force. He stuck out his hands to absorb the force of the collision.

She grabbed him in a fierce embrace. Her yelling continued. "You promised! You promised no more chances. No more sacrificing. No—" Jennifer's protests grew softer and less coherent. They became sobs.

All the tension of the freeway chase and the caves had returned in an instant. It was now draining from her through the yelling, the sobbing, and the tears.

The two stood in the alleyway with arms wrapped around each other and with Jennifer's head pressed tightly against his chest.

There were no more words.

The alley grew quiet until Peterson, who was standing over Abdul, began barking commands. "Get this man out of my sight. Use whatever restraints you need to keep him under control and..." Peterson paused, "if anybody tries to read him Miranda rights, I'll have that man's badge. Is that clear?" Peterson paused again.

Heads nodded.

"Good."

Peterson's words sounded distant to Lee as he pulled Jennifer close. Other words—words from Jennifer's favorite "hymn" found their way from yesterday into his conscious mind. He whispered them softly to Jennifer, *"Two hearts are one now."* He didn't need to interpret. She was a bright woman. She could deal with his double meaning.

Peterson, behind them, spoke their names to someone. "As long as they stay over there don't bother Lee and Jennifer. They're not disturbing any evidence."

Lee placed his hand under Jennifer's chin and tilted her head upward forcing her to look at him. The large brown eyes could be piercing, but now they were filled with tears. There was no trace of anger left in them. He pulled her close and kissed her forehead.

Jennifer's words began again, but they came softly now. "I had already made my decision. In my mind it was done."

"I'm glad it was only done in your mind." He paused. "So now that you know who you belong to and where you're ultimately going, you're fearless?"

"It doesn't work that way."

"What you mean, Jenn?"

"The fear was still there, but love overcame fear. Then you spoiled it all." Once again the fire returned to her spirit and the piercing look to her eyes.

"Oh, brother." He prepared for round two. "I don't think I spoiled it. I just tried to do the same thing you tried to do. You can't blame me for it. But I think God had a better plan all along."

Her piercing look softened. "And what's the better plan, bringing Peterson here at just the right instant?"

"That's part of it. But I think He wanted some new relationships to have time to grow, maybe for a lifetime."

Lee's words absorbed Jennifer's remaining emotions like a sponge. She became limp in his arms.

He supported her for a few seconds.

When Jennifer stood on her own again she kept her arms around him. "Please tell me it's over—that everything is OK, now."

"It is all OK now, Jenn, except for one thing. Maybe I'm the one who should get angry this time. I saw what you were doing—what you actually did. Do you know how much you scared me?"

"You deserved every bit of it. That's exactly how I felt in the cave when I saw what your plan actually meant. You wanted to toy with the goons for revenge instead of getting safely off from the mountain. Don't ever do that to me again."

"I'm sorry I made you feel that way. But you don't have to sacrifice yourself for me to prove you love me, or to prove anything at all. You don't have to do anything, but just be you."

"I wasn't sacrificing myself to prove that I love

you, but *because* I do. You ever heard of Jesus, Lee?"

There was a warm smile on Jennifer's face and he was already basking in it.

Jennifer was right where she belonged in his arms.

He sighed and relaxed. The stress of their latest brush with death was over. After all they had endured it was hard to believe there would be no more nerve-wracking stress.

The spunky Jennifer Lee had completely fallen for was back. Maybe being forgiven would make granting forgiveness a little easier for her. He hoped so.

Jennifer, with her arms still around him, looked into his eyes and spoke softly. "Lee, one of these days I'm still going to kill you."

He tensed for another round, but the playful look in her eyes told him the fight was over.

"I'll bet you say that to all the guys."

"No. I've never wanted to kill any guy but you, Lee."

"How silly of me." He looked down at her eyes. "I thought I had a reason to be jealous."

She met his gaze. "You don't have to be jealous. I only say that to people I love."

"If I remember correctly that was the plot of a horror movie."

"I'm not a character from some horror movie, but I probably should confess that I have a big problem."

He brushed a wisp of hair from her face. "What's that?"

"I tend to use hyperbole for effect. You know, a bit too much."

"Yes, you do. But as long as it's only hyperbole I forgive you." He kissed her forehead.

"If it wasn't hyperbole you wouldn't get the

chance."

Another smile told him, at least for the next few moments, all was forgiven. Once again everything was good and warm between Jennifer and him. One thing he had learned with Jennifer, any current state of affairs could only last a few moments. In this case, a few wonderful moments.

24

Lee peered into her eyes and saw that the confident, spirited, vibrant Jennifer had returned.

"You hungry?"

"Famished. Where would you like to go?"

"How about a good, old-fashioned American diner? After this weekend I don't want anything foreign for a long time."

He took her arm. They walked slowly around the building towards the parking lot. "Sounds great. I know just the place."

Jennifer pointed towards the entrance to the church building. "It seems like a lifetime ago that we walked into the church."

"In one sense for you, it was. In walked the old Jenn and now the one with the new life is walking out." He opened the driver's side door.

There was no protest.

Jennifer appeared deep in thought. A calm, peaceful look appeared on her face. It only enhanced her beauty.

Maybe the Source of her peace was now completing the wonderful creation He had in mind when He first thought of creating Jennifer.

In a few moments the vehicle rolled through the parking lot. When it reached the street, Jennifer stopped the big SUV. "OK, where is this great place?"

"Hang a left. Go about two miles and the

restaurant will be on our left."

"This is an American restaurant, right?"

"The best one I know of. I wouldn't give you a bum steer. If you like steak the restaurant won't either."

Jennifer smiled. "No, you wouldn't. I guess you have always pointed me in the right direction."

Double meanings, maybe triple meanings this time, but he no longer minded them.

Jennifer was silent.

He waited for a few moments, and then broke the silence. "You look like you're trying to digest everything we've experienced in the last forty-eight hours."

She glanced at him and flashed him a smile. "Something like that."

Lee cleared his throat. "Let's see if I can sum it up for you. Two days that combined the worst of times with best of times, in the nick of time—a tale of two days."

"So Lee Brandt thinks he is Dickens?"

"No. Lee Brandt thinks he is hungry. The restaurant is one block ahead on the left."

Jennifer looked up at the big neon sign. "The All American Diner? I guess you really meant it when you said the greatest American place."

"Wait until you taste the food. Nothing but the best American food for my all-American woman."

She gave him a warm smile. "All-American woman is the best compliment you could have given me. I love this country. That's why I do the kind of work that I do. But things like the plot we stumbled onto—I'm afraid for the future of our country."

"I'm afraid too. If I hadn't called Howie, or if I had

turned down his offer for your help I hate to think about what might have happened. One success just emboldens more terrorists."

"I'm glad you didn't turn down Howie, too. I hate to think of all I would have missed out on. God and—"

"God already had his eye on you. He would've drawn you to Himself, regardless. That's part of His sovereignty."

Jennifer sat still and stared out the windshield. "Sovereignty. Does that mean something like people can't thwart His will?"

Lee nodded. "That's a good way to put it."

Jennifer laid her hand over his, clasping it. "And it was a very good way He worked things out for me and for us, don't you think?"

"Very good, except I would've gotten the SWAT team to the church on time. About five minutes earlier. I don't ever want to come that close to losing you."

"Lee, we wouldn't have lost each other forever. Not after this morning."

"No." He frowned. "Not forever. But I kind of like the thought of spending our lives together here on planet Earth, first."

Her almond-shaped eyes squinted as she peered at him. "Do you want to explain exactly what you meant by that?"

Lee braced himself for some kind of outburst. "No, I don't."

Instead of giving him an outburst of anger she gave him a coy smile. "I didn't think so. But, at least you didn't lie to me. Now, let's go in and have some of that All-American food."

Forgiveness? Is that what she just gave me?

When Lee escorted Jennifer through the door into

the diner it seemed they entered into another time. "Well, what do you think?"

Jennifer stopped, smiled, and scanned the large, open room. "Black-and-white checkered floor, red vinyl seats, booths along the wall. Looks like America, circa nineteen fifty-five."

He gestured towards an empty table in the middle of the room. "My mom and dad have tried to describe what life as a child was like in the late fifties and early sixties. They said it was an innocent time. Listen to the music, Jenn."

Words that said only one person could make this world seem right came from the big jukebox in the corner creating a soothing atmosphere.

Jennifer sighed as she walked towards the table. "Yes, being here almost makes me forget what we experienced this weekend. Life in twenty-first century America. Not an innocent time."

After seating Jennifer he sat opposite her and folded his hands on the table. "I wish we could recapture some of what that generation had." Lee's gaze wandered down the directory of songs listed on the mini-jukebox on their table. "Maybe we can. And look, Jenn, there's not a single British group listed. Only American music. Is this American enough to suit you?"

Jennifer had already opened a menu. "It's perfect," she replied, as she turned to address the approaching waiter. Before Lee could speak, she placed their order. "Prime rib and potatoes with a garden salad for both of us, please. You can choose our drinks, Lee."

Her order stopped any protest he might have voiced. Once again he smiled and let his gaze rest on Jennifer. "Two cherry cokes, please."

After the waiter left with their order Jennifer leaned forward onto the table and looked into Lee's eyes. "OK. Now that we've ordered the next item on the agenda is—"

"Is you. In some ways I feel like I know everything about you, yet in others almost nothing at all. There's a lot more I want to know."

She reached across, unfolded his hands and took one of them. "As long as I get a turn at this too, you can ask away."

"You can have your turn, but only if you go easier on me than you did coming home yesterday."

The warmth in her eyes conveyed the message, even before her words reached him. "You don't have to worry about that. You already passed my test."

"Just for your information I like my test better." Today the subject of tests brought no protest from Jennifer. "Now. Questions. Let's see. Have you ever been convicted of a felony?"

"Come on. I have a Top Secret SCI clearance. What do you think?"

"OK, what about traffic tickets?"

"None."

"Well you should have gotten several. I've seen you speeding, running red lights—"

"You're not funny. I'm squeaky clean and you know it. "

"You already told me your dad died. But what about your mom?"

She stared across the room. "She moved back to Hawaii not long after Dad died." Her gaze came back and met his. "It was a hard time for us all."

He placed his free hand over hers. "I'm sorry you had to experience that." He paused. "Your last name is

Japanese. Is your Mom Japanese, too?"

"My dad was Japanese, as was nearly fifty percent of the island population eighty years ago. No. Mom is Hawaiian."

"That explains it then. Two beautiful races of beautiful people and you get—"

"Look, we're not going to talk about appearances today."

He was looking and he couldn't help thinking about her appearance. Nor could he forget her temper, which seemed to have mellowed.

Maybe she just oscillates between aloha and hara-kiri.

A penetrating look from Jennifer made him fear she had read his thoughts. He decided continue the questioning while he still had the floor.

"OK. Do you have relatives here on the mainland?"

"Yes. My grandfather on Dad's side lives about two hours south of here."

"What about brothers and sisters?"

"Despite what you think I'm not an only child. I have two younger sisters—much younger than me. Both live on Oahu with Mom."

He wanted to ask about her sisters. How much younger? What were their ages? He changed his line of questioning. "Did you like church today?"

"You know I did. After the sermon, the last song really grabbed my heart. But tell me something, does your church always test a new Christian's faith by threatening their life? That's pretty brutal."

He laughed. "No, it doesn't. If it did though, you would've passed with flying colors. But can we please stick to more pleasant subjects?"

"Do you mean like the looks we're getting from

three-fourths of the people in the restaurant?"

"Are we—"

"Yes. We're in a fishbowl here."

As he glanced around the room eyes from nearly every table were focused on them.

He supposed Jennifer was drawing much of the attention.

But they had definitely been recognized.

"Do you want to leave?"

"No, but I'm not comfortable with—"

"I think we just need to break the ice. Then we might find this place will warm up nicely." He looked to his right and smiled. "In fact, there's an icebreaker headed our way right now."

Jennifer looked up into the smiling face of a white-haired gentleman. She was fidgeting—definitely uncomfortable.

He related to people more easily than her. He would frequently take her out of her comfort zone. Maybe it would be a good thing.

Lee looked into the man's face and smiled, but Jennifer continued to shift uncomfortably in her chair with the uninvited attention.

"Miss Akihara, Mr. Brandt, please pardon my intrusion on your dinner. But a lot of folks here tonight want to thank you two for what you did for all of us. Now, I know the news never tells things as they really are and probably some of what you did will never be told to the public. But, may God bless you for your service to us and to the USA."

It sounded like the media told more than they should have even known. Those prying reporters probably found a loose tongue or two in Kerbyville.

Jennifer smiled at the heartfelt thanks.

Lee stood and reached for the man's hand. "Thank you sir. You're a veteran, aren't you?"

"Yes, son. I was in the Army. Infantry, World War II."

"I thought so. Jennifer and I owe you a much deeper debt of gratitude for your service."

"Did you serve too, son?"

"Air Force, five years. I served in Iraq briefly. But due to my job I was mostly stateside."

After only a few short words he felt the bond between the two men, one-half century apart in age, being cemented. When the two vets embraced as men do, patting each other on the back, he noticed the music had stopped.

Applause broke out throughout the diner. Above the applause, he heard, "God bless you and God bless the USA."

He smiled as he watched Jennifer being swept into the sense of community warming the atmosphere of the restaurant. It was the right thing for the World War II vet and for Jennifer, too.

Her face relaxed and she was smiling now.

With a simple greeting and an embrace as catalysts, the diner morphed from a room partitioned into many isolated family groups to the atmosphere of a family reunion.

He shook his head and chuckled. "I think sometimes celebrities would be better off if they didn't run and hide. Just think of the bonds they could build with their fans."

With friendly chatter creating a comfortable background he turned his attention back to their dinner, which was now being served, and, of course, to Jennifer.

"Did you know how the conversation would go when you stood up?"

"No. But by the man's age and bearing I was pretty sure he was a World War II vet so who was I to turn him away? He was a hero because of a heroic choice. We just got terrorized into the part."

"Don't remind me, please. I don't feel like a hero either, just a survivor. But I heard you tell him you were in the Air Force."

"Yes. Five years. That's where I got into meteorology. They sent me to school for a year to get my degree."

"So you didn't go here to the University of Washington for your undergraduate work?"

"No. I went to Texas A&M."

"Do you mean Lee Brandt is a real, live Texas Aggie?"

"Guilty as charged. And no Aggie jokes, please."

"No jokes." She took his hand and squeezed it. "But since it's my turn now I've got some more questions for you."

"As Peterson says, 'OK, shoot'."

She gave him a mock frown. "You just had to say that, didn't you?"

"Sorry. Bad joke."

Her smile replaced the frown. "You're forgiven—"

"Jenn, I think you're growing soft. Did God do that to your heart?"

"Maybe God and a certain meteorologist I know."

"Good for them. Maybe now I can forget about running through the flea cave and—"

"Don't count on it. If you ever lie to me, Lee Brandt, you'll find yourself in a cave on Iron Mountain in your underwear. And I can get you there pretty quickly."

"So I've observed. But, if you ever drive that recklessly again you'll probably kill us both."

She ignored his comment. "Now. Regarding your family, tell me about your parents, brothers, and sisters."

"Mom and Dad retired early. They live in Arizona. Lake Havasu City. I have a brother living in New Mexico and a sister who married and moved back east. Ohio. It's not the East Coast, but that's back east to me."

"Birth order, Lee. Out with it."

"You sure can be demanding. I'm the oldest."

"I knew it. But you know something?"

"What, Jenn?"

Jennifer looked down at her dinner. "We'd better eat our steaks before they get cold."

"Good idea. Can't live on love."

Her coy smile returned. "How do you know? Have you ever tried?"

"Never had the opportunity before."

"Before what?"

"Before you. But let's not try that now. I'm hungry."

25

Lee couldn't believe he had found someone like Jennifer.

After she dropped him off at his apartment and he unlocked the door and entered, it struck him that he had been with Jennifer for nearly all of the past forty-eight hours. Walking into his apartment used to feel like coming home. Now it felt empty and he felt incomplete.

At 8 p.m., he sat propped up on his bed contemplating the changes Jennifer had made in his life...and several changes he still needed to make. His phone rang.

"Hello...7:30 a.m.?...With the CEO?...You want Jennifer at the afternoon office party?...I'll make sure she's there." It was his second-level manager, Barry's boss.

He picked up the post-it adhered to the nightstand beside his bed and glanced at the number before keying it in. He didn't need to. He'd memorized it twenty-four hours earlier.

"Hello."

"It's Lee, Jenn. I guess you really did give me your phone number."

"After our twenty-hour date and after today does it still surprise you?"

"After this weekend I don't believe anything about you will surprise me."

"How should a woman take that?"

"I just meant that now that I know how amazing you are nothing you do will amaze me."

"You're really pretty good at pulling your foot out of your mouth. But you've probably had a lot of practice."

Despite the mile between their apartments he could see the smile on her face. "Thanks a lot. The reason I called is you need to meet me at the parking lot at North Fourth and Park Avenue about five 'til one tomorrow afternoon."

"You've got to be kidding. No. Been there, done that, Lee. I don't think it's a safe place to meet."

"It's safe for people who drive black SUVs. I'm the one who should be worried. I'm in the white sedan."

"I won't be armed and I won't chase you. I promise." There was laughter in her voice.

"So, you'll be there?"

"Silly guy, of course I'll be there."

"I'd better go. The CEO called me with orders to brief all of upper management about the incident early tomorrow morning."

"Do you think you'll get much flak about some of the things we, uh, rather, I did?"

"If I do I think I've got enough political and news-media clout at the moment to give it right back to them. I wouldn't be giving them anything they didn't deserve. After all, they were the ones who created the conditions exploited by the terrorists."

"Will you give them flak like you did with Barry yesterday? That was impressive, Lee. Thanks for standing up for me."

"You deserved it. Besides, it felt pretty good to me, too."

"Goodnight."

"Goodnight. See you tomorrow."

Tomorrow couldn't come soon enough. Walking into his work area with Jennifer on his arm was something he couldn't wait to experience. As he lay on his bed he planned his presentation for the CEO. He was still fleshing out his indictment for outsourcing a critical computing system when his thoughts faded from gray fuzziness to darkness.

****

Monday afternoon Lee slipped through the turnstile and watched a black SUV roll up to the gate shack, where Randy stood on duty. When Jennifer's window slid down he heard Randy's nervous voice.

"Is that you in there, Jennifer?"

"Who did you expect?"

"Right now any black SUV makes me pretty jumpy."

"I'm really glad you're OK. Lee and I were worried about you after hearing all the shooting."

"Thanks. But you'd better park that thing. Here comes Lee."

By the time Jennifer found a parking spot, Lee stood alongside the SUV. "Grab my hand, Jenn. Let's give Randy something to talk about."

She took his hand. "You don't waste any time, do you? You're a smooth operator, Lee Brandt. Tricking me into holding hands."

"Aren't I." He squeezed her hand, while the two walked towards the gate shack.

"Brandt," Randy's voice sounded across the parking lot. "Is this a social visit or work?"

When they approached the gate shack, he replied. "Both, Randy."

"Remember last time?" Randy smirked at them. "Are you sure you want to do this again?"

He smiled. "Very sure."

Jennifer filled out the visitor's form and then produced her driver's license.

Randy remained quiet through the rest of the guest-badging process. But as the two walked towards the turnstile the security guard cast his slur.

"Really robbing the cradle aren't you, Lee?"

Jennifer dropped his hand, whirled, and leapt in front of Randy. "Look, idiot! I'm twenty-five years old — at least as old as you. I have a master's degree, and I work for the government. The only one robbing the cradle was the doofus who hired you!"

Randy's face turned white and then back to a glowing shade of embarrassed pink.

Jennifer ended her stare with her coy smile. "Gotcha, Randy."

Randy's rigid posture relaxed when he recognized Jennifer's feigned anger. "Whew. Lee, I'd hate to see what it's like to really make her mad."

"Believe me, that's not something you want to do. I've done it."

Jennifer returned to his side and looked up with her squinting frown. "Was that a Christian thing to do?"

He took her hand again. "Certainly. God has a sense of humor, too. After all, He created the duck-billed platypus."

"How'd your briefing go this morning?" She squeezed his hand.

"It went well. You impressed upper management

with your work and our story intrigued them. We're not in any kind of trouble. On the contrary, we're headed to a party in our honor. Barry didn't plan it. That's no surprise. It was his boss's idea. The CEO will be there and he wants to meet you to thank you in person."

"What about the wrap-up session Peterson mentioned yesterday?"

"That'll be after the party. In Joe's office on the first floor."

Lee escorted Jennifer to the large second-floor conference room. He held her arm when they stepped into the doorway.

Loud applause greeted them.

When Jennifer stepped in far enough for everyone to see her, the room grew silent. He was growing accustomed to Jennifer's effect on men the first time they saw her.

National Aerospace's CEO started clapping again. The applause spread throughout the room. The party began. But Jennifer's face still held the gaze of every man in the room. He couldn't blame them.

His second-level manager seated the honored couple with the attending managers.

Lee would have preferred sitting with the IT staff. But he and Jennifer were being honored. He shouldn't complain.

As the applause quieted, the CEO of National Aerospace remained standing.

Lee cringed at this turn of events. This man, politician that he was, could not stop talking once he started.

"Mr. Brandt, I think you should introduce your friend to everyone here, the girl who—"

"I am not a girl, sir."

Please say he didn't say that. CEOs should know better.

Jennifer, seated one chair away from the CEO sprang from her chair and faced him.

"I am twenty-five years old. I hold a master's degree in computing security. I work for NSA and sometimes the FBI. Last weekend, sir, I believe I saved your bacon."

After her outburst, Jennifer turned to the audience. "My name is Jennifer Akihara and now you know me."

Lee heard several of his co-workers trying to stifle their snickers. Some weren't successful. Others failed utterly. This left the tense audience not knowing what to expect.

No matter. The CEO was too stunned to notice, yet.

The audience began to laugh and he sought to legitimize the object of their laughter by focusing it on Jennifer, the person, not on her words or the CEO. He stood. "That, my colleagues, is Jennifer. Now you certainly *do* know her."

Laughter erupted.

The festive atmosphere returned.

A few moments later Jennifer whispered into Lee's ear, "I'm so sorry. I lost my temper. What should I do?"

"Find a chance to get his attention. Then tell him what you just told me. It'll be OK. Just do it." He placed his hand on her arm. "But later," he gave her a big smile, "you need to ask God to take that temper away." His suggestion drew a stare and a frown.

"But He's the one who gave it to me."

He held her gaze. "Yes, but the Lord giveth and the Lord taketh away."

Jennifer relaxed and smiled. "I think you just don't

want me mad at *you* anymore."

He took her hand under the table. "And I think you're right."

The incident had ended well. He hoped the afternoon would also, because some important issues remained.

Nearly everyone in the room wanted to shake Jennifer's hand and thank her for her role in protecting their corporation. From the small talk he verified that most people in the room knew few details of the threat. Lee had learned in the morning meeting that Computing Security and the CEO did not want to reveal the nature of the threat until the company had deployed an adequate defense for this type of cyber attack.

For the next thirty minutes Jennifer seemed to enjoy the party, but after a serving of cake and ice cream she began fidgeting in her chair.

"Jenn, you look like you're ready to head down to Joe's office."

"You've got that right. There are too many gawking eyes in here."

He leaned close to her. "I saw you apologize to the CEO."

She nodded.

He lowered his voice to a whisper. "I don't think he felt as gracious as he acted. You don't become CEO of a Fortune 500 company unless you're a good politician. The other requirement is a large ego."

She returned his whisper. "I agree with your assessment. Can we please leave now?"

"As soon as I can courteously extricate us."

Five minutes later, the two headed down the stairs towards Joe's office.

When they reached the bottom of the stairs, she glanced at him. "How far do you suppose they've gotten in the investigation?"

He shrugged. "Don't have a clue. They've had less than forty-eight hours since we briefed them on Saturday afternoon. Here's Joe's office." He knocked on the door. "Let's go in and find out."

Joe opened the door before Lee finished rapping on it. "Jennifer, Lee, come in. We're going to move to the inner office now."

He had heard about this more secure area, used for sensitive discussions, but he'd never been inside it.

Was his lack of a current clearance going to exclude him from part of this meeting?

Joe shoved a paper at him. "First, Lee, you need to read and sign this form."

The form answered his question. Joe's document authorized him to have specified access to information regarding the investigation. The justification was based upon the extent of his existing knowledge, his role in unraveling the plot, and his previous high-level clearance.

When they entered the room Jennifer began speaking before she sat down. "Sorry about forgetting to mention the paper with the addresses on it, Peterson. I left it in the driver's side door pocket."

Peterson sat at a table with a small stack of papers in front of him. "No problem. We found it Saturday afternoon shortly after locating your car. Your labels were completely explanatory—compromised PC IP addresses and hacker IP addresses."

Jennifer sat down and leaned forward, but shifted her gaze to Stewart. "Were you able to gain further intelligence using the IP addresses?"

Stewart nodded. "Yes, we were. I'm not authorized to tell you how, or who was involved, but we've added several organizations to our incident-response team since Saturday. Suffice it to say the cooperation between this group of terrorists and the Mexican drug cartels has ended for now and—"

Jennifer focused on Stewart. "What about this terrorist organization's collaboration with the cartel in Colombia?"

Obviously Jennifer wanted to complete her agenda before anyone could steer the discussion in another direction.

Peterson cleared his throat. "I'm not at liberty to provide you with names and specific locations. However, we do have that information. A plan was implemented to neutralize the current effort by the terrorists' hackers. Columbia. Well, we have a lot of work to do before cleaning up the mess there. But for now, we believe the existing Colombian ties to terrorist activity in Mexico have been snipped."

Lee had an agenda, too. He turned towards Joe Morrison. "Have you been able to determine the extent of the computing threat within National Aerospace?"

"Yes, Lee. Well, nearly. We're currently completing a scan of every company computing device. We used the notes Jennifer made and the file she provided to create a network-wide scanning program. So far, we've found five infected machines, all in the commercial part of the house. Nothing on the military side. US-CERT helped us with the scanning program. You'll hear more about it over the coming week."

He stared at Joe, hoping he'd heard correctly. "So their access to sensitive information was, for all practical purposes, nil. That's good news."

Joe nodded. "Sure is. And based upon a phone call we got about an hour ago regarding somebody saving our CEO's bacon, I believe she did just that."

With everyone grinning at her Jennifer sighed. "Good. But after outsourcing DEDS to an offshore company I wouldn't mind if it sizzled in the pan for a few seconds."

Joe's grin became audible. He snorted.

Peterson shuffled the papers in front of him until he looked satisfied with the one on top of the stack. "About the three suspects. Jennifer. As you know, the woman is dead, and suspects number two and three are in custody. They have not been given Miranda rights. We want to keep the military trial option open. While it remains to be seen whether they will be tried in a military or civilian court, I'm told that, barring outright acquittal, they will never be free again. Only the imposter appears to have taken your actions personally and sought revenge. Though I don't know how you can distinguish revenge from jihad with someone holding to his worldview. Regardless, his attempts on yours and Lee's lives will not go well for him. You both will be asked to testify against the perpetrators at some time and in some court. But other than testifying, you and Lee can get on with your lives."

Peterson stood. "Well, that's about all we—"

Jennifer glanced at Lee then back to Peterson. "We would still like to know how a SWAT team arrived at the back of the church at just the right time."

Peterson slipped his papers into his briefcase. "The third suspect, the vengeful one, stole a car and drove to the city limits. Police started asking questions and we got a rough description of the man we thought was the perpetrator. A nearby neighbor indicated a man might have entered the back of the church before sunrise on Sunday morning. We got the information a few minutes before he got to you two. Captain Lewis arrived and began listening to what was going on inside about the time the three of you moved to the door. We only had one opportune moment to intervene and fortunately, Lewis was able to take advantage of it."

Lee stared across the room at the wall. "But if the timing had been off a second or two I don't think we would have made it."

Jennifer took his hand under the table. "I think that's where our Lord's sovereignty took over."

A smile spread across his face. "And I would say you're probably right."

Peterson cleared his throat again. "As a precaution we may have both of you watched for a while." He focused on Lee. "So, Lee, don't do anything you wouldn't want on video, or in a report."

"Hey, Peterson, why did you single me out? Jennifer is the one who needs to hear that."

"You're digging a hole, Lee. Be careful or I'll plant you in it."

He glanced at her, and then back to Peterson. "Can't you lock her up for all the threats you've heard her make to me in the last three days?"

"Sorry. That's not the FBI's jurisdiction," Peterson locked his briefcase. "I think you need one of three people to help you, a minister, a justice of the peace, or an undertaker."

"What about a counselor," Stewart suggested.

"Been there, tried that. Doesn't work," Lee

quipped. "So I would opt for one of the first two." He glanced at Jennifer and was surprised to see the calm, beauty-enhancing look he noticed for the first time on Sunday.

When the meeting ended several things were evident. One battle in the war on terror had been won thanks to Jennifer, the FBI, NSA, a local JTTF, and its member police departments.

Joe had performed admirably and with integrity as he guided National Aerospace through a crisis.

A second battle, one for Jennifer's allegiance, was won by God, Himself.

The third battle, a battle for his heart, was won by a woman with a fiery spirit, a new growing relationship with Christ, and a demand for total honesty. She hadn't only won the battle, but also the war. The time had arrived for him to run up the white flag. One unsettling question remained.

What might total surrender to Jennifer require?

26

When they left the building a little after 2 p.m. Lee avoided the turnstile by the gate shack. He doubted Randy wanted another encounter with Jennifer today.

When they entered the parking lot a warm wind blew out of the southwest. When the breeze swirled around vehicles in the parking lot Jennifer's hair danced around the perimeter of her sunlit face.

Jennifer was too beautiful to describe.

Nothing mattered except not letting this woman slip away from him.

He needed more time with her and he needed it now. "Did you eat any lunch?"

"Cake and ice cream."

"That's what I thought. Would you like some lunch now?"

She brushed a strand of hair from her eye. "After dessert, I don't think so."

He had more suggestions. A lot more. "What about coffee?"

"Sounds great, but I'm driving."

He forced a frown. "So you don't want to ride in a plain vanilla car anymore?"

"No. The SUV is like rich chocolate. We're bonding. Let's hit the coffee shop drive-through. You probably have to get back to work pretty soon, anyway."

"Not today." He sighed and smiled. "I'll tell you

about it later."

Jennifer's eyes narrowed. She watched him from the corners of her eyes. "Sounds mysterious."

They climbed into the car and drove in silence for a few blocks to the nearest coffee shop. After negotiating the drive-through Jennifer pulled into a space in the parking lot.

She took a sip of coffee and placed her drink in the cup holder. "Lee?" There was a long pause. "I have something to tell you."

"OK. What is it?"

"What we did Friday night. It helped National Aerospace. It helped the USA and it made me feel like I accomplished something good, not just something that furthered my career."

This was an unexpected direction. There was nothing threatening yet, but he was concerned. "It should make you feel good. It *was* good. You're one of only a handful of people in the world who could have accomplished all that you did."

"Lee, I'm just going to cut to the chase. Getting my Ph.D. is not going to help me one bit. I'll waste eighteen to twenty-four months jumping through the university's hoops to learn a few things I can easily learn on my own. Then there's all the campus politics that impacts Ph.D. students. You know, 'Do we really want to put our stamp of approval on this young woman?' You have to prove to them you're worthy of their approval by doing things you'd rather not do. I'll have to teach geek courses to underclassmen. They can be an obnoxious bunch." Jennifer paused. "So, well...I've decided to take the job offer from NSA." Jennifer picked up her coffee cup.

He wasn't sure what to say. He remained quiet

while they both sipped coffee.

Jennifer's decision worried him. NSA Headquarters was almost three thousand miles away.

"Does this mean you'll be moving across the country to Maryland?" He stared down at his coffee cup avoiding her eyes and dreading her answer.

Jennifer put a hand under his chin and gently lifted his head. She was looking into his eyes and smiling. "Lee Brandt, sometimes you can be pretty dense. No. I'll be working locally. Quite a bit of the time with Howie. I can't tell you more about it than that. But regarding Fort Meade, only occasional trips."

"So you'll be staying here, then?"

"That's what I just said. Do you think I haven't meant anything I've said or done these past three days?"

"No."

Jennifer always meant everything she said, excluding perhaps the hyperbole about murder.

He sensed a smile growing on his face as hope returned. "But if you really meant everything...in that case, I think I'm dead."

"Only if you ever lie to me. Remember this. I won't let you get away like the gunmen did."

"I've got something to tell you, too."

"The mysterious thing?" Jennifer was frowning.

"It's related. The reason I don't have to be back to work at any certain time today is I've resigned from National Aerospace, effective in four weeks." He paused. "I don't enjoy developing computing systems for corporate America anymore. Most guys who do systems-development work burn out when they're about my age. I've decided to go back to my first love, meteorology."

"Oh." Jennifer stared down at her coffee cup, rotating it in her hands. A coy smile crept onto her face. "Maybe I was wrong, but I thought I was your first love."

"I was only talking about work."

"Who says I'm not work?"

"You are a lovely work."

Jennifer ignored his comment. But her smile was morphing to a frown. "And where will you be doing this meteorological work?"

"I have two friends, Dale and Jerry, who've been after me to join the meteorological consulting firm they've been laying the groundwork for this past year. There's a strong possibility our first big contract will be either directly or indirectly with NSA, if our facilities and personnel can meet their security requirements."

Jennifer raised her gaze to his face. "How did you manage to swing that?"

"Did I ever mention I was an intelligence analyst in the Air Intelligence Agency before I got a degree in meteorology and became a weather officer?"

"No, Lee. There's still a lot you haven't told me about yourself. But even if you once worked with NSA how are you going to get them to run a top secret clearance for you?"

He peered into her eyes. "Don't you know you don't get NSA to run anything?"

Jennifer smiled at his use of her words.

He continued his explanation. "My old DOD Top Secret SCI clearance was recent enough to be reinstated with an update to the background check. They really want our firm to help them with some weather-related issues so NSA is willing to make the clearance update happen."

Jennifer's voice softened as she looked into his eyes. "So you'll be working locally, too?"

"If you're not leaving neither am I. Since our weather firm will work closely with NSA for the duration of the contract I'd bet our paths will cross at work."

Jennifer's expression morphed again from serious to coy. "What about when we're not at work?"

"Are you suggesting—"

"What I'm suggesting," Jennifer looked down, exhaled sharply and then returned her gaze to his eyes. "Is that I would like to date you if you would just ask."

"So you trust me, then?"

"Yes, I trust you."

He slipped his palm over his left knee. "Jennifer?"

"Yes, Mr. Brandt?"

"Come on, Jenn. This is a serious question."

"OK. That's better. What's the question?"

Looking through his frown he studied her face. "Why me? What made you trust me?"

She reached across and began tracing the contours of his left hand with her fingers. "Nothing made me. But do you really want to know?"

"Yes, I'd like to know how I got it, because I don't want to lose it."

She took his left hand and squeezed it. "Are you sure you want to hear this? Because it's going to be the whole story—the good, the bad, and—"

"Yes. I want to hear it."

"Remember you asked for this. When Howie brought me into his office I saw your eyes. You were all gaga just like the guys who give me grief. Don't you even try to deny—"

"Maybe I was. But you have no idea what it's like

for a guy to have you sprung on them with no warning." He pounded his right knee. His coffee geysered from its sip hole and slopped onto his right hand. "It's...it's—"

She pulled her hand from his and tossed him a tissue. "Sounds like it's IQ-nulling."

"Something like that." He draped the tissue over his right hand.

"But you seemed to recover quickly enough to your full one-hundred forty-five, right?"

Where did that number come from?

His gaze jerked up from his hand to her face. "You didn't really do what I think you did. Did you?"

"I don't know what you're thinking. But I do know I hacked the university's admin database and got the goods on Mr. Lee Brandt."

"But I thought you were Miss Honest."

"Like I said before I'm not perfect. But I did check you out. Admissions records, high school transcripts, complete with IQ scores, college grades, reports from your master's committee, everything. No way was I going to have this kind of reaction to some gaga-eyed guy without knowing all about him. But you were clean, with a one hundred forty-five—"

"What kind of reaction are we talking here?"

"The kind I've never had before and that's all you need to know."

He reached for her hand. "What if I need to know more?"

She slapped at his hand. "Don't push it!"

"What about the trust?"

Her voice softened. "That came when I saw you were putting my needs ahead of yours. Even putting my life ahead of yours. I knew I could trust you when—"

"A few minutes after we entered the cave, right?"

She stared at him. "I should kill you right now. You knew and yet you manipulated me into disclosing personal stuff that—"

"Stuff we'll share for the rest of our lives—the truth about ourselves—truth we'll never use to hurt each other. Remember what I told you about a relationship with God being intimate, like between a husband and wife—nothing in between?"

Her eyes widened and she reached for his hand. "Is all that just informational, or are you asking me to marry you?"

He wrapped his hand around hers. "Something like that."

Go on, man. Tell her.

"Something like what?"

Yeah. Tell her.

"Something like—well, you know I told you I don't date?"

Jennifer's head tilted down. Her hand went limp.

His own brain had ganged up on him. Both sides. He just needed to say it. "But I would like your permission to ask the appropriate person in your family if I may court you."

It's about time.

Yeah. It's about time.

It was time. Probably the only time he would ever have.

Jennifer had raised the bar to an impossibly high standard. Despite her fiery temper she stood head, shoulders, and much more above any woman he had ever met. Life without Jennifer—he couldn't let that happen.

Her face tilted upward, but it wore a frown. "Does courting mean we can't date?"

"Technically, we can't date, that is, not until we've begun courting. Then we spend a lot of time together getting to know each other better."

She smiled warmly. "Courting sounds a lot like dating, but it also sounds very—"

"First I need your answer. May I, you know, with the intent that we marry whenever we're finished courting?"

Her coy smile crept onto her face. "What do you think we've been doing for the past," —she glanced at her watch—"sixty-five hours and forty-five minutes?"

"If you knew that's what was happening why didn't you help me out a little? You can be pretty hard on a guy."

"You had it easy. Most guys just get pepper-sprayed. But who said courting me was going to be easy?"

"If you're counting this past weekend something tells me it won't. But I hope the coming months are a lot less eventful than the last sixty-five hours and forty five minutes."

Jennifer cocked her head. "Are you sure that's what you want? It would make for a pretty dull courtship, don't you think?" She studied his face. "Besides, what makes you think we're talking months, anyway?"

Had he heard correctly? "Not talking months? Then let's just elope now."

"You're jumping the gun. First shouldn't you get permission to court me?"

"Yes."

But she said her father died two years ago.

"Who do I need to talk to?"

"My grandfather. But I need to warn you, be careful never, ever to cross Granddad. He never forgives anybody for anything."

"Sounds a lot like his granddaughter."

"C'mon, Lee. You can't complain about me until I make you run the flea cave in your underwear."

27

Tuesday afternoon, March 21

As momentous as the last four days were for Lee Tuesday was even more important. The day wouldn't determine if he lived or died, like Friday, Saturday, and Sunday. Rather, it would determine whether he lived wishing he had died.

Jennifer sat beside him in the white sedan. She didn't appear to be worried. But she knew this unforgiving man who lived one hundred miles to the south. Their two-hour drive down I-5 held no terror for her.

He grew more nervous with each mile. There was so much on the line and he had never met Jennifer's grandfather.

To top it all off he had to show up in a rental car which had none of the class of his '65 Mustang convertible. "I was sure you would want to drive your SUV down here."

"No, Granddad should see you in your car."

"But I don't have a car." Would that count against him?

"This car is fine for visiting Granddad. Have you gotten any word from the insurance company about your Mustang?"

He nodded. "Yeah. Sort of. Since it's a classic car, they'll pay me a comparable price for it. I didn't like their first set of numbers so I ran my own comps. My Mustang was worth more than I thought. The insurance company will come around after they see my numbers. They're a good company and I've been with them since I was sixteen."

"So are you looking for another '65 Mustang convertible?"

"No. My Mustang was really too light to be safe. It could literally jump off the road if you hit the gas pedal on wet pavement." He shot her a glance.

It drew her attention.

"My next car will be carrying some precious cargo so I want a big, safe car. What would you like me to get?"

"I don't think I've ever been called cargo before. I'm not sure how I feel about that. But I do like classic cars." Jennifer paused. "I think you should get whatever you want. You don't have to ask me."

"But I'm thinking you'll probably be spending some time in my new car, too."

Jennifer rested her hand on the console. "You mean when we're not in the SUV?"

"Yes. We won't be in it all of the time, will we?"

"No, I don't have to drive all of the time." She drew an X on the console with her index finger. "Didn't most of those old cars have bench seats, you know, so a guy's date could slide over to the middle?"

"Yes. But we have seat belt laws, now. What were you suggesting?"

She moved her hand to his shoulder. "Only that I like the bigger classic cars. But remember this. I don't park."

"That's good. I don't, either." He glanced at her and grinned. "Why park in some dark spot when you can kiss in a cave?"

Her coy smile appeared. "So that's why you dragged me up that mountain and climbed down the rock to the hidden cave. To take advantage of me."

"If I remember correctly, it was you who took advantage of me."

She pulled his right hand off the wheel and held it. "I'm guilty. So what do you plan to do about it?"

Her hand felt warm, soft. He pulled it to his lips and kissed it. "One thing's for sure. I'll never forget that kiss. Bad things tend to happen to me in caves."

"Bad things?" She pulled her hand from his. "Maybe I should take back the kiss."

He reached for her hand and missed. "I didn't mean the kiss. I meant—"

Don't air your dirty laundry, man.

She grabbed his hand and gripped hard. "You need to tell me the rest. No secrets, intimate, nothing in between, remember? Something happened to you in a cave. Something you'd rather not tell me. Out with it."

"It was just a little panic attack."

She squeezed his hand even harder. "You took me to the caves to keep me safe and you have panic attacks in caves?"

"At least I'm not afraid of heights."

She shook her head. "Just afraid of depths."

He exhaled sharply. "OK. Once my buddy and I lost our light while climbing a cavern wall. One like you and I climbed. A smelly one with foul air. When the light went out I couldn't breathe. I panicked and bailed out into total darkness. Didn't have a clue how high up I was. Fortunately, it was only about fifteen feet. Fortunately, I have strong legs and ankles." He looked at her face. "Fortunately, I survived."

Jennifer was silent for a few moments. "How many people have you told about this?"

He sighed. "Just one. You."

"Lee?"

"Yeah."

Her grip on his hand eased. "I love you. I'm glad you told me and I'm really glad you didn't freak out on me Saturday."

Someday I'll tell her how close I came.

"Me, too. And I love you, too."

Jennifer watched him out of the corners of her eyes. "Besides liking classic cars there's something else you should know about me."

"What's that?"

"I'm carrying." Jennifer patted her side.

"Carrying what?"

"As they say in the movies, I'm packin' heat. I do most of the time. I meant to tell you before now."

"So you really meant it all those times you said you'd kill me?"

"No, unfortunately I wasn't carrying it last weekend."

"Uh, I'd say that was fortunate."

She gave him a wide-eyed frown. "Fortunate? We could have defended ourselves."

He shook his head. "I can't think of a single scenario where we could've tried to use that kind of gun on those people and survived to tell about it. You know, the thing called superior fire power. If we even once stopped running and tried to fight we wouldn't be here having this conversation."

"You're right. Maybe it was a good thing I left it in my locker in the computer lab Friday night."

"Do you mind telling me why you carry a gun?"

Her hand went limp. "I had a bad experience with a stalker."

He slipped his hand from hers and caressed the back of her hand. "I'm so sorry you had to endure something like that. Where's the guy now?"

"He's in prison. And, well, he walks with a permanent limp."

He grabbed her hand. "Jenn, you didn't shoot—"

"Shoot him? I certainly did. He's lucky I didn't try to kill him. I usually hit what I aim at."

He interlaced their fingers. "So it's not all hyperbole, then?"

Her coy smile returned. "As I said, I've never wanted to kill anyone but you."

So Jennifer had one notch on her gun. He smiled and, at the same time, felt sorry for anyone who threatened her.

I'll make sure no one ever gets the chance.

He sensed it was time for a change of subject. "How about a red and white '62 Impala convertible?"

Her head snapped around towards him. "A big car—did you really find one?"

"Yes. It's been restored, but it's not completely stock. The engine has been bored out a bit. Oh, they added air conditioning and a nice stereo, too. And..." He grinned. "No bucket seats."

"Just remember, courting or not, I told you my rules."

"I know. We don't park." He paused. "I've only told the man I'm interested. What have you heard about your car?"

"Only a rumor. Stewart's trying to pull some strings to give me the SUV to drive while I work for NSA. Just like you said he's using it as bait to get me to sign the work contract. He has some reasons for wanting me on board quickly."

He chuckled. "Oh yeah, about two hundred of them." He paused for a moment. "So it was a good thing you and the SUV bonded?"

"I think so."

He pushed up on the turn signal. "Well, this next exit is ours. How do we get to your grandfather's place?"

Jennifer looked out the passenger-side window. "We're exiting onto the main drag through town. Just stay on it. In about two miles, there's a Dutch Brothers coffee shop. Turn right. It's a couple of blocks to his house."

He cancelled the signal and braked to a slower speed. "Dutch Brothers? I didn't know Dutch Brothers had come this far north."

"That's because you didn't see my two full Dutch Brothers' cards. The ones I rescued from my car at the Kerbyville police station."

He chuckled again. "So, you're a heavy drinker too? But you can't say I drove you to it."

"No. But it would be nice if you did."

He stopped for a red light. "I can take a hint. OK, it's Dutch Brothers on me."

"You say the nicest things."

He glanced at Jennifer and found it hard to pull his eyes back to the road. "Could we live without coffee?"

"Probably not. But you wouldn't live without telling me the truth." Jennifer's mouth was smiling, but her eyes said there was an element of truth to her words.

He reached out for her hand. "Please don't start

the threats again. I thought our relationship was beyond that."

"Our relationship can never be beyond threats." She squeezed his hand. "It is beyond murder, though. I think."

He pulled his hand free to make the turn into the Dutch Brothers drive-through. "Great. What am I getting myself into?"

When he stopped in the lane, Jennifer's hand gently turned his face towards her. "Please look at me." She paused.

He glanced her way.

"No...I mean really look."

He peered deeply into Jennifer's eyes. For the first time he could read them like a book.

She unmasked everything for him to see.

What she revealed took his breath away. "If I can see those eyes every day you can threaten me as much as you want to." He remained lost in her eyes until a car behind them honked.

Jennifer nudged him with her arm. "Time to move ahead, and...you've got yourself a deal."

"But I've got to get past your grandfather to seal it. Except for the forgiveness part, he's not like you, is he?"

She gave him her enigmatic smile. "You'll see."

In a few minutes the two drove up to Jennifer's grandfather's house as they sipped the last of their coffee.

He slipped out of the car, walked to Jennifer's door, and opened it for her. While they walked towards the front door, Lee took a deep breath, exhaled, and tried to relax.

"You worry too much. Just be yourself."

She wasn't overly concerned about this meeting.

Maybe he should relax, too.

Her grandfather was over seventy. But when he welcomed them at the door Lee noticed he had the bearing of a much younger, athletic man.

After the introductions Jennifer occupied herself by miscellaneous cleaning tasks in the kitchen, while her grandfather invited Lee outside to the deck.

The rain had stopped about noon and the sky had cleared. The sun felt warm on this first day of spring. Lee hoped it was also the first day of spring in the life of Lee Brandt.

Her grandfather turned to face him. "So now we talk, Lee."

"Yes, sir."

He studied Lee's face. "Jennifer tells me you saved her life. You were going to sacrifice your life for hers. Is that true?"

He dipped his head. "Yes, sir, it's true. But it's not the whole story. We saved each other's lives several times. But on Sunday when the gunman tried to shoot us Jennifer dove at him to give her life for mine."

Grandfather turned his head and watched Lee from the corners of his eyes. "I think there is more to tell. What did you do?"

He took a breath and exhaled. "I dove for him, too, at the same time. Since I'm stronger I got to him first. But fortunately for us that's when the SWAT team entered."

Grandfather still watched him from the corners of his eyes. "I see. And you are telling me the truth?"

And you'll kill me if I'm not, won't you?

"Yes, sir." He nodded again.

Grandfather turned and faced him squarely.

"Jennifer told me you wished to court her. What do you mean by that?"

How should he explain this? "When two people think they both have found the person they should marry they spend a lot of time together, getting to know one another much better. Then, if they believe God is leading them to marry they do so at the end of the courtship."

"I see." Grandfather looked directly into his eyes. His gaze was nearly as piercing as Jennifer's. "What if God says yes, but I say no to the marriage?"

He gets right to the point, like his granddaughter.

"Then, sir, I would respect your wishes. But I would probably knock on your door every week to see if you changed your mind. I love your granddaughter. What we went through together compresses time. I know Jennifer as well as if we dated for quite a while." He stopped and waited for a response.

Silence.

After an uncomfortable minute Grandfather spoke. "I like your answer, Lee. But I have one more thing to tell you. I have a sixth-degree black belt in Karate. Though I am seventy-two years old if you ever hurt Jennifer, physically or emotionally, I will kick your head off."

This was guy talk. He knew how to answer it. "Sir, if I ever hurt her I'll give you a free shot at my head."

Grandfather pressed his palms together. "It is done, then. You two go court. But hurry, because I am an old man who wants to know his great-grandchildren. Jennifer is my oldest grandchild, oldest by several years. Have I made myself clear enough?"

He smiled. "Yes, sir, you have."

It was clear enough. But how would he break the

news about great-grandchildren to Jennifer? He smiled.

It might be fun.

It might be dangerous.

I know, left brain. I know.

Mr. Akihara smiled and shook Lee's hand. Apparently, their business was concluded and he was now courting Jennifer Akihara with certain stipulations about offspring.

When he entered the house Jennifer smiled when she saw he was smiling.

Her grandfather looked at both of them and smiled.

A short time later when Lee and Jennifer left her grandfather's house to drive home they were still smiling, though he hadn't told Jennifer the outcome of his talk with her grandfather.

He pulled out of the driveway still withholding the outcome of the courting discussion. When he glanced her way, Jennifer's smile was gone. Evidently, her patience went with it.

"I know Granddad would want you to tell me about your discussion. But when did you plan to do that? Just before the wedding?"

He cleared his throat. "Well, I was trying to think of a good way to break the news."

"Come on. Granddad would never have turned you down. So tell me what—"

"You're right about one thing. He did say yes to our courtship, but that's not all he said."

Jennifer's smile returned. "OK. Tell me the rest."

"Are you sure you want to hear this?"

"Just tell me now, or I'll—"

"I know. You'll kill me. But the real question isn't

about what you say you'll do. It's whether you'll do what your grandfather wants."

Jennifer's eyes narrowed, squinted, and then opened wide. "Spit it all out. Now."

He placed his hand on her arm. "OK. OK. First, he told me if I ever hurt you, he would kick my head into orbit."

She slid her arm until their hands clasped. "That sounds like Granddad."

"Then he demanded that we court quickly so you can give him great-grandchildren soon. He was very emphatic on that point."

"Oh." Her mouth froze in the shape of the letter she spoke.

He studied her face. Two intensely pink areas appeared on Jennifer's light brown cheeks. After a few moments she spoke in a soft voice. "Then I guess it's official. We're courting and the courtship may not be very long."

Jennifer placed her left arm on the center armrest and leaned her head onto Lee's shoulder. There was a warm, sweet silence in the car.

For Lee Brandt, life indeed was good.

Only one more item of business to handle.

He slowed a few blocks before they reached the freeway and pulled into the coffee shop parking lot. When he turned off the engine Jennifer still leaned against his shoulder.

He lifted his right arm and draped it around her. "I've heard it from your grandfather, but I need to hear the official answer from you, Jenn. If we're going to do this—"

"Of course we're going to do this." She sat up and slapped his knee. Jennifer's intense stare returned. She aimed it directly at his eyes.

Lee returned her gaze trying to match its intensity. "Then we need to seal the deal."

"And just how do you propose we do that, Mr. Brandt?"

He continued peering into the depths of her brown eyes. "Something like what we did on the Benson's front lawn, but without the audience."

She smiled warmly. "Hmmm, 'Sealed With A Kiss.' Wasn't that one of those oldies songs?"

"Would you please shut up and start sealing?"

Jennifer sealed the deal very, very nicely.

Author's Note

The setting of this book is never disclosed sufficiently for the reader to determine exactly where the scenes take place. Though the Pacific Northwest is alluded to, and a metropolitan area that sounds like Seattle is described, you won't find the streets and areas referred to on a map—not in the orientation described in the book.

The other areas used in the setting actually do exist in the Pacific Northwest. However, I have woven two interesting geographical areas together, though they are actually about three-hundred miles apart. Yes, the caves exist, and I know them intimately—too intimately. All of this obfuscation was done purposefully because I did not want the book to sound like an indictment of any American person, business, or organization. We are not the enemy.

Please note that National Aerospace was meant to represent generically an important American industry, the defense industry, and not any existing corporation.

The law enforcement and anti-terrorist organizations mentioned all exist and cooperation between them is improving as they attempt to combat terrorists and organized crime. Unfortunately, terrorists are also improving their cooperation and extending that collaboration to organizations like the drug cartels. The threats presented in the book are very real. The author has personally investigated a similar security breach.

Most of the characters in the book are composites of people the author has known, thus they are fictional. However, many events depicted in the lives of the characters have actually occurred. Though some of these events may tug on the bounds of believability, most have actually happened, albeit in somewhat different contexts than in the book's plot. For example, you can email the author and inquire about the flea cave if you want to know what it feels like to be shrink-wrapped in fleas and jump into a creek fed by melting snow to wash the little devils off.

As for the two main characters, Lee Brandt and Jennifer Akihara, people like them do exist. That is as much as I will reveal about this extraordinary couple, except for one last comment. If enough people enjoy reading about Jennifer and Lee, they will be back very soon with the danger level ratcheted up several notches.

Thank you for purchasing this Harbourlight title. For other inspirational stories, please visit our on-line bookstore at www.pelicanbookgroup.com

For questions or more information, contact us at titleadmin@pelicanbookgroup.com.

Harbourlight Books
The Beacon in Christian Fiction™

May God's glory shine through
this inspirational work of fiction.

AMDG